The Lone Star Love Potion

An American Farce

by Michael Parker

I0591600

A Samuel French Acting Edition

SAMUEL FRENCH

FOUNDED 1830

SAMUELFRENCH.COM

ISBN 978-0-573-62678-4   Printed in U.S.A.   #14209

MUSIC USE NOTE

IMPORTANT BILLING AND CREDIT
REQUIREMENTS

THE LONE STAR LOVE POTION was first produced at the Delray Beach Playhouse, Delray Beach, Florida, on July 17, 1996, with the following cast

MELODY	Diane DuMar-Nelson
JARVIS	Michael Parker
PATRICE LEADLEY	Charlotte Sherman
MICHAEL LEADLY	Marc Streeter
MR OAKFIELD	Charles Newman
TAMMY-JO HARPER	Marjorie Hines-Gagnon
MARY-LOU WINSTON	Carolyn Gordon

Directed by Randolph DelLago
Designed by Ann Cadaret

The action of the play takes place in the main house of the L P Circle Ranch in Texas, owned by the late Mr Edward Stancliffe

Time The Present
ACT I A late afternoon in spring
ACT II Later the same evening

CHARACTERS

MELODY (age 20-30) The late Mr Stancliffe's maid is, in fact, in the one profession she should not have chosen She drops things, she breaks things If there's a wrong way to do something, she'll find it! Pursued throughout the play by Michael, she resists his advances in a variety of ingenious and hilarious ways She is an endearing character loved by audiences
A natural comedienne, young, perky, sexy

JARVIS (age 50+) The late Mr Stancliffe's butler He can be English or American, but should not be Texan A pivotal character who is deeply involved in the mystery of the love potion and around whom most of the circumstantial humor seems to evolve He remains throughout the quintessential butler, always calm, always in control
Suave and serious, but with a sparkling dry wit

PATRICE (age 30-50) The late Mr Stancliffe's niece and heiress to his estate She has suffered through her husband Michael's infidelities for many years In a surprising turn of events, she too becomes involved in the "affair" of the love potion and reveals a romantic and passionate side of herself
Elegant, attractive, sophisticated

MICHAEL (age 30-50) Patrice's husband and an inveterate lecher He sets his sights on Melody (and any other female that is breathing) but is repeatedly rebuffed and struck "where it hurts most " A comic character who is at the center of most of the visual sequences
Brash, loud, self-centered Not very likeable

MR. OAKFIELD (age 40+) A short, balding, overweight lawyer who gives the impression of a quiet, mild-mannered man until he too is caught up in the excitement of the love potion He

spends most of ACT II trying (unsuccessfully) to find a vacant
bathroom in a series of classic comedic sequences which leave
the audience roaring

A typical lawyer, perhaps a little officious and pompous

TAMMY-JO (age 25-40) The neighbor from across the creek, sur-
prisingly mentioned in Mr Stancliffe's will Deeply involved in
the love potion plot, she appears to be a fairly straight character
for most of the play, but later has her "moment in the sun" as
she turns into a sensuous temptress

Very Texan, very beautiful

MARY-LOU (age 30-50) A serious, matronly ornithologist doing
research on the ranch Her character of the drab, dowdy, unat-
tractive woman in blue jeans, boots, poncho etc is changed by
the love potion into a voluptuous seductress in black lace teddy,
fishnet hose, high heels etc The fact that she has no idea how to
play this role puts her in the middle of some of the funniest sequences

Plain, then glamorous Conservative, then sexy Shy, then outrageous

ACT I

(The curtain rises on an empty set It is the living room and study of the Texas ranch home of the late Edward Stancliffe We see a bedroom R, and a living room L The wall between is cut out except for the U S connecting door, which has a light switch below it on the R side The room is, in fact, a study with wood paneled walls that has been turned into a bedroom It is small, and contains only a double bed against the R wall, with a nightstand and bedside light below it Above the bed, on the R wall, is the door to the powder room There is a window in the center of the U.S wall)

(The living room is typical of a Texas ranch, with cow skins on the floor and animal heads on every wall U S center is a small stairway to a landing which runs the length of the living room The U S wall on the landing contains three doors R is bedroom 1, center the bathroom, and L is bedroom 2 The landing continues off stage L to the west wing bedrooms U S on the L wall is a double hinged door to the kitchen, with a light switch below it, and D L a double front door with a light switch on the wall above it L C is a couch with a low coffee table below it, and a reading lamp behind it against the L wall R C are two low backed easy chairs with a small table between them)

(The landing rail has bric-a-brac fastened to it, branding irons, firearms and an enormous pair of iron tongs on the R side of the steps Below the landing, to the R side of the stairs, is a

table which serves as a bar It is totally cluttered with glasses, bottles, etc L of the stairs is a low bookcase which has among its books a set of encyclopedias Every spare inch of wall has something on it, old cowboy paintings, guns in frames, horse trappings, etc It almost looks more like a museum than a home)

(After a few moments, MELODY enters from the kitchen Age 25-35, she is pretty, attractive, and is immediately recognizable as the maid She is wearing a black, pencil, wrap-around skirt with a small white apron, a white blouse, black hose and high heeled pumps She is carrying a tray containing six glasses, a small vase of flowers and some silverware She crosses R towards the drinks table and as she comes just below the stairs she trips over one of the cow skins She staggers R , then D S a little, desperately trying to maintain her balance With the tray held precariously above her head, she eventually falls backwards over one of the low backed chairs, and ends up lying on her back with her legs in the air, but the tray still balanced Breathing a sigh of relief, she manages to return to a standing position, and carries the tray to the drinks table She tries to find room to put it down, but the table is too cluttered with glasses, bottles, etc She tries to clear a space with one elbow, but to no avail Eventually she raises one leg, and by holding the tray with one hand and balancing it on her knee, she manages to free the other hand As she starts to clear a space on the table with the free hand, she wobbles on the one leg, the tray tilts dangerously and starts to fall She tries desperately to save it, but the tray falls, she falls, everything goes with a tremendous clatter Amazingly, nothing breaks, as everything on the tray is made of plastic)

(JARVIS, hearing the noise, enters from the kitchen He is the epitome of the English butler Age perhaps 50, graying, ramrod straight, serious, rarely smiling and always very formal He wears dark pinstripe pants, a long sleeve white shirt with French cuffs and a dark vest and tie He has a dish towel in his hand)

JARVIS *(Crosses R and helps MELODY to her feet)* Melody my dear, are you alright?

MELODY *(Gets up and straightens her clothes)* I'm O K thanks, but I'm afraid I've done it again

JARVIS Never mind Come on, I'll help you *(He starts to pick up glasses, etc)* At least nothing got broken

MELODY *(Picks up the tray)* That's because you only ever let me carry plastic things

JARVIS We both know that's a very sensible rule for you Melody Now come on, Mr & Mrs Leadley will be here any minute and we can't let them see this mess

(As MELODY picks up each glass she gives it a cursory wipe with her apron and puts it on the table JARVIS picks each one up and gives it a thorough polish with his towel before replacing it on the table, exactly positioning each one in line)

MELODY Oh Jarvis, I'm so sorry about this, it's just that I'm very nervous

JARVIS I've told you before, there's nothing to be nervous about

MELODY That's easy for you to say, Mr Stancliffe always promised to take care of you when he died, but by this time tomorrow, I might have no job, and no home

JARVIS *(Stops clearing up, and takes MELODY's hands in his)* Melody, haven't I promised to take care of you? *(She nods)* Well then, there's nothing for you to worry about

MELODY When will we find out?

JARVIS Today in fact Mr Stancliffe's lawyer is coming here to read the will He should be here any minute

MELODY You know, Mr Stancliffe probably left everything to Mrs Leadley She is his only living relative

JARVIS You forget that Mr Stancliffe was a very wealthy man He had lots of assets besides this ranch and the twenty-thousand acres I'm sure he didn't forget us, so stop worrying Just remember, we agreed, you leave everything to me Now, have you finished getting the west wing suite ready?

MELODY It's all done Clean sheets, towels, everything

JARVIS Good, we need to make sure Mr & Mrs Leadley are comfortable We want them to feel right at home

MELODY By now it probably is their home

JARVIS Melody, please don't say things like that Until we've seen the will, we just don't know I was Mr Stancliffe's butler for 29 years and we were very close He knew that my dream was to own this place one day, and I have absolute faith he did the right thing

MELODY Right for who? You or Mrs Leadley?

JARVIS We'll see, in any event I have a feeling it's going to be an interesting day Ah, there's a car *(He heads toward the front door)* They're here Bring the coffee in will you

(MELODY exits to the kitchen with the empty tray as JARVIS opens the front door and looks out   It is raining heavily as PATRICE dashes in She is an attractive woman in her middle thirties, wearing a two piece suit, blouse, conservative accessories and high heeled shoes She has a raincoat draped over her shoulders and a newspaper held over her head She carries a purse which she puts on the coffee table)

PATRICE Hello Jarvis Boy, it's really coming down now

JARVIS Good afternoon Mrs Leadley Welcome to the L P Circle Ranch *(He takes the raincoat and newspaper from her)*

PATRICE Thank you Jarvis

(Enter MICHAEL, age 40-50, he is a nondescript looking man, whose appearance belies what he really is, a lecher with the morals of a soap opera leading man He is wearing gray pants, a blue blazer, shirt and tie, and a raincoat He carries two suitcases which he puts down just inside the door)

JARVIS *(Closes the door)* Good afternoon, Mr Leadley

MICHAEL Oh, hi Jarvis *(He takes off his raincoat which he hands to JARVIS)* Boy-o-boy! I'm telling you, when it rains in Texas, it really rains

JARVIS I think I'll just hang these things in the laundry room
If you'll excuse me for a moment, I'll be right back and show you to
your rooms *(Exit to kitchen)*

PATRICE Thank you Jarvis *(Wandering around the room)*
You know this room looks exactly the same as it did when I was a
kid I don't think Uncle Edward moved anything in thirty years

MICHAEL Well it gives me the creeps, when it's ours I want to
get rid of all these dead animals

PATRICE Michael, you don't know Uncle Edward left us the
ranch

MICHAEL Of course he did, you're his only relative, who else
would he leave it to?

PATRICE *(Opens the study door and looks in)* Well, that's
strange, they put a bed in the study

JARVIS *(Who has returned from the kitchen and overheard the
last remark)* Yes madam For some time before Mr Stancliffe went
into the hospital, he was having trouble negotiating steps, so we
turned his study into a bedroom, and I just haven't had time yet to
move the bed out and put back the furniture *(He comes D L to pick
up the suitcases and moves up the steps to the landing)* If you would
follow me madam, I've put you in the suite of rooms in the west
wing. This way please

*(PATRICE follows him leaving the center door ajar MICHAEL
follows PATRICE JARVIS and PATRICE exit to the west wing,
but just before MICHAEL exits, MELODY enters from the
kitchen, so MICHAEL stands U L on the landing and watches
her She is carrying a tray with a coffee pot and mugs As she
negotiates the swing door from the kitchen, her skirt is caught in
it She twists and turns, and the wrap-around skirt comes right
off, held firmly by the door She is now seen to be wearing black
lace tap pants, garter belt and stockings She comes D to the
coffee table and bends down to put the tray on it MICHAEL,
unseen by MELODY, creeps down behind her, and as she bends,
he grabs her derriere MELODY shrieks and jumps away)*

JARVIS *(Who has returned from the west wing just in time to see this)* Feeling a little left behind are we sir?

MICHAEL I - er - she - er - I was just helping her

JARVIS *(Looking down his nose)* Yes sir So I see Perhaps you should go and "help" Mrs Leadley sir

MICHAEL Right - good idea - yes I'll go right away She'll need some help with the bags Yes - good idea -

(He moves up the steps, past JARVIS and exits to the west wing)

JARVIS What in heaven's name happened this time?

MELODY My skirt got caught in the kitchen door

JARVIS *(Retrieving the skirt and bringing it to her)* I honestly don't know how you do it

MELODY *(Putting on the skirt)* Well, at least I didn't spill the coffee

JARVIS I suppose we should be thankful for that

MELODY You know, when they were here last time he tried to grab me One of these days I'm going to punch him in the "you know whats " He's a dirty old man

JARVIS Nevertheless, he does seem to have some success with members of the opposite sex

MELODY Oh sure If you shoot at everything that moves, you're bound to hit something Someone needs to teach him a lesson

JARVIS That may be so my dear, but he is Mrs Leadley's husband, so, until we know what's in the will, and where we all stand, let's just keep the peace shall we *(There is the sound of a car outside)* Ah, there's another car That'll be the lawyer, Mr Oakfield *(Crosses D L to the front door)* Would you tell the others he's here please Melody

(MELODY exits to the west wing JARVIS opens the front door It is still raining Enter MR OAKFIELD He is a middle aged, balding, slightly overweight, and wears glasses He is carrying a briefcase and an umbrella, which he closes in the doorway He is wearing a hat and a raincoat over a dark business suit, etc

JARVIS takes the umbrella and hat and closes the door)

JARVIS Mr Oakfield Good afternoon sir

OAKFIELD Good afternoon Jarvis, right?

JARVIS Yes sir *(Helps him off with the raincoat)* Here, let me have that

OAKFIELD What a day Are Mr and Mrs Leadley here yet?

JARVIS They arrived about five minutes ago sir

OAKFIELD Good, and Miss Harper?

JARVIS I beg your pardon sir?

OAKFIELD Miss Harper from the Circle-Cross ranch across the creek Surely you know her?

JARVIS Indeed I know her very well sir I just didn't know she was expected here today

OAKFIELD Yes, of course Well, I asked her to be here at four o'clock

JARVIS I see But no, she's not here yet *(Enter MICHAEL and PATRICE from the west wing They come D S They are followed by MELODY who stays U S just below the steps)* Ah Mrs Leadley, do you know Mr Oakfield?

PATRICE Yes, in fact we've met several times How are you Mr Oakfield? *(They shake hands)* Do you remember my husband?

OAKFIELD Of course How are you Mr Leadley?

MICHAEL I'm fine thank you *(They shake hands)*

JARVIS Right If you'll excuse me, I'll just get these wet things put away There's fresh coffee on the table *(He moves U S towards the kitchen, stops and turns)* I hope you don't mind plastic mugs, it's - er - a sort of tradition in this house

PATRICE Thank you Jarvis *(They all sit OAKFIELD L end of the couch, PATRICE the L chair and MICHAEL the R chair)* Melody, perhaps you'd like to pour the coffee

(MELODY takes a step forward, then stops and looks at JARVIS who is by now in the kitchen door)

JARVIS *(Turns abruptly)* That's probably not a good idea

madam *(Patrice frowns at him and starts to say something)* Just
trust me please madam

*(PATRICE shrugs, gets up, crosses to the coffee table and pours
JARVIS signals to MELODY to follow him and they both exit to
the kitchen)*

PATRICE How do you like it?
OAKFIELD Black please *(She hands him a mug)*
MICHAEL What's all the secret about the will? I thought you
only had, you know — "the reading of the will" in mystery novels
and theatrical productions

*(PATRICE pours two further mugs, gives one to MICHAEL, takes
one herself, then returns to her chair)*

OAKFIELD *(Laughs)* There's really no secret The will is to be
read in everyone's presence simply because Mr Stancliffe specifically
instructed that it was to be done that way
MICHAEL He always was as nutty as a fruitcake
PATRICE Michael!
OAKFIELD I can assure you he was perfectly sane sir
However, I would go along with "a little eccentric "
MICHAEL Well, what are we waiting for? Let's get on with it
OAKFIELD As a matter of fact, we are waiting for someone
(He opens his briefcase, takes out a paper and reads) A Miss
Tammy-Jo Harper
PATRICE Who's she?
OAKFIELD Apparently she owns the neighboring ranch, just
across the creek
MICHAEL I take it then that she's - er - mentioned in the will?
OAKFIELD Yes sir
MICHAEL I see
OAKFIELD You do know, don't you, that your uncle was
extremely wealthy?
PATRICE I've never really thought about it, but yes, I guess I've

always known I mean this ranch is enormous.

OAKFIELD If it's not an impertinent question, do you mind if I ask what was the source of this wealth?

PATRICE I don't mind you asking at all, because I have absolutely no idea where or how he made his money I know he was in South America a lot when he was young and I've always thought it was something to do with that

OAKFIELD I see How interesting

(Enter JARVIS from the kitchen He comes down to the front door)

JARVIS Excuse me, but there's another car just pulled up

(He opens the front door, we see it is still raining Enter TAMMY-JO, she is a strikingly beautiful woman, age 25 to 40. She is wearing a loose, baggy, poncho-style slicker and a cowboy hat which she takes off and hands to JARVIS She is now seen to be wearing cowboy boots, a mid-calf length blue denim skirt with an ornate silver belt, and a checkered shirt with pockets)

JARVIS Good afternoon Miss Harper Let me have your coat please *(He turns to the room)* May I introduce Miss Tammy-Jo Harper, Mrs Patrice Leadley

(Everybody shakes hands)

PATRICE Hello
JARVIS Her husband, Michael
MICHAEL Nice to meet you
JARVIS And, of course, Mr Oakfield.
OAKFIELD Hello
T-JO Howdy everyone
JARVIS Let me get rid of these things and organize some more chairs I won't be a minute

(He exits to the kitchen)

OAKFIELD Please sit down
T-JO Thank you

*(TAMMY-JO sits on the couch R end OAKFILED stands D L with
his back to the front door, PATRICE and MICHAEL return to
their chairs)*

MICHAEL How well did you know Mr Stancliffe?
T-JO Well, I didn't see too much of him in the last year or so I
guess he was really sick but I've known him just about all my life I
suppose
MICHAEL I see
T-JO When I was a kid I used to ride my horse over here all the
time When my Daddy was alive he and Mr Stancliffe were like, you
know, best buddies
MICHAEL I see

*(MELODY enters from the kitchen carrying two straight chairs She
gets briefly wedged in the kitchen door, then crosses R As she
gets to the cow skin, she stops, very deliberately walks around it,
then puts the chairs down between the couch and the L chair
She turns D S , smiles at everyone and returns to the kitchen)*

PATRICE Well Miss Harper, it seems that Uncle Edward has
left you something in his will
T-JO Oh How exciting
PATRICE Please help yourself to coffee
T-JO Thank you

(She pours a mug)

MICHAEL Can we go ahead and read the will now?
OAKFIELD We need Jarvis and Miss Melody Ah - *(JARVIS
enters from the kitchen)* Jarvis, can Melody join us too please?
JARVIS She'll be in in a moment *(He stands just below the
stairs)*

OAKFIELD *(After an awkward pause)* Chair?

JARVIS *(Looks at the chair, then looks back at MR OAKFIELD)* So it is!

OAKFIELD No, no, I meant would you like a chair?

JARVIS Thank you but I already have several of my own

OAKFIELD I mean, would you like to sit down?

JARVIS Ah! Yes Indeed I would Thank you sir *(He sits on the L straight chair)*

(MELODY enters from the kitchen and crosses R to sit next to JARVIS She trips over the cow skin, staggers R and ends up in JARVIS' lap He helps her up and into the other chair JARVIS and MELODY then just smile at everyone)

OAKFIELD O K I think we might begin *(He takes papers out of his briefcase and stands with his back to the front door to read)* This is the last will and testament of Edward William Douglas Stancliffe *(He looks up over his glasses)* I am, of course, familiar with this document as I helped Mr Stancliffe to prepare it With your permission therefore, I will cut out all the legal mumbo-jumbo, and just deal with the bequests In any event, copies of this document will be made available to you later, should you require them O K Here we go then Firstly there is a trust fund whose basic function is to provide income to maintain this ranch and pay the salaries of Melody and Mr Jarvis Should Melody leave or be dismissed she would receive a lump sum payment of $50,000 from the trust

MELODY *(Leaps to her feet, punches the air and screams)* Yes!

(JARVIS gets her seated again and they both smile as Oakfield continues)

OAKFIELD In the case of Mr Jarvis, Mr Stancliffe states that in recognition of his many years of devoted service, his salary is payable as a pension for the rest of his life There then follows a rather strange and complex deed of trust, which in simple terms states that, while the ranch is bequeathed to you Mrs Leadley, Mr Jarvis may live here for the rest of his life Furthermore, you may never sell any part of it without the express permission of Mr Jarvis during his lifetime

PATRICE Does that mean that after Jarvis - er -

JARVIS *(Stands)* Rings down the final curtain madam?

PATRICE Well, yes

OAKFIELD You own the ranch with no restrictions

PATRICE I see Thank you

(JARVIS sits)

OAKFIELD The ranch that is, with one very small change Mr Stancliffe makes a bequest to Miss Tammy-Jo Harper of a small tract of land, some 400 acres known as the Goat Creek Bottom He goes into a long rambling explanation about water rights on the creek, which I must admit I never fully understood

T-JO Oh, I understand all about that When my Daddy was alive he had a sort of unwritten gentlemen's agreement with Mr Stancliffe giving our cattle access to Goat Creek The Goat Creek Bottom gives us a way to get there without crossing anyone else's land

OAKFIELD I see

T-JO That sure was generous of him

OAKFIELD Excellent then To continue All of the other assets, which are somewhat modest compared to the value of this ranch, he leaves to his only living relative, Mrs Patrice Leadley *(He looks up, around the room)* Oh, I nearly forgot, there's one other thing There's a limited liability company called Amelixco Incorporated The company is in good standing but does not appear to have any assets The shares are bequeathed as follows Mrs Leadley 25%, Mr Leadley 25% and Mr Jarvis 50% All I can tell you is that the company has a registered formula with the U S patent office, which, of course is secret At the time Mr Stancliffe drew up this will, I tried to persuade him to divulge the formula to a representative of my firm He declined, saying, if I remember, it was too dangerous And that just about does it

MICHAEL That's really strange

OAKFIELD You will, of course, all have to come into my office and sign all the papers, but there's no hurry, any time in the next two or three weeks will be fine Now, I really should be on my way *(He closes up his briefcase)* I'll leave a copy of this for you Mrs Leadley *(He puts a file on the table)* If you have any questions please call me

JARVIS *(Stands)* Melody would you get Mr Oakfield's coat please

(MELODY exits to the kitchen JARVIS picks up one chair and follows her)

OAKFIELD It's been a pleasure to meet you Miss Harper

T-JO *(Stands and they shake hands)* Thank you Please be careful crossing the low bridge on the creek, the water level can rise real fast

(Enter MELODY with the raincoat She comes down and tries to help OAKFIELD put it on One sleeve is inside out He puts his arm in that sleeve, MELODY twists the coat so that other sleeve faces the right way He tries to put his arm in but it doesn't work They stop, extricate his arm and start again She gets her arm in one sleeve, they end up both half in the raincoat JARVIS has followed MELODY from the kitchen carrying OAKFIELD's umbrella and hat He comes D L)

JARVIS Excuse me Would you hold this for a second please? *(He hands the umbrella and hat to TAMMY-JO and then gets MELODY untangled)* There we are sir *(He gets OAKFIELD into the raincoat then hands him the umbrella and hat)*

OAKFIELD Thank you Now don't forget you all need to come into my office

MICHAEL We won't forget Thank you *(Shakes hands)*

OAKFIELD Goodbye Mrs Leadley

PATRICE Goodbye, and thank you *(Shakes hands)*

(JARVIS opens the front door and OAKFIELD exits We see it is still

raining JARVIS closes the door)

JARVIS Melody, perhaps you could clear away the coffee things *(MELODY looks at him in panic)* Go on It'll be alright

(MELODY picks up the tray)

T-JO *(Putting mugs on the tray)* Here let me give you a hand
MELODY *(Quickly pushes the tray into TAMMY-JO's hands)* O K I'll get the door for you

(She rushes U S trips over the cow skin, keeps her balance and holds open the kitchen door TAMMY-JO, carrying the tray, exits to the kitchen followed by JARVIS MELODY smiles at everyone and exits backwards into the kitchen Immediately there is a tremendous crash)

PATRICE Do you get the feeling Jarvis isn't telling us something about Melody?
MICHAEL *(Deep in thought)* You know, there's something about that Amelixco company that I don't get If it has no assets, why bother to keep it going? It doesn't make sense
PATRICE Well I'm sure I don't know It's probably just another of Uncle Edward's little peculiarities
MICHAEL I guess so

(Enter TAMMY-JO from the kitchen She is putting on her slicker She is followed by JARVIS who carries her hat)

T-JO I need to get going It's still raining, and at this rate it won't take long for the low bridge to wash out *(She comes down to PATRICE)* I hope we'll be seeing each other often, now that we're going to be neighbors
PATRICE That'll be nice
MICHAEL Yeah! That'll be real nice

(JARVIS, who has come down to the front door, gives MICHAEL one of his sternest disapproving looks, opens the front door and hands TAMMY-JO her hat It is still raining)

T-JO I'll see y'all around then

(She dashes out into the rain JARVIS closes the door)

PATRICE Is everything alright in the kitchen Jarvis?

(She sits on the couch, L. end)

JARVIS Just a minor mishap madam Excuse me

(He exits to the kitchen)

MICHAEL *(Sits on the couch, R end)* Well, we've just about got the whole works
PATRICE Yes, it looks like we did
MICHAEL The only problem is we're stuck with Jarvis
PATRICE Oh, he's alright
MICHAEL I'm not saying he isn't I'm just not sure I want to live with him
PATRICE That's a point
MICHAEL What do you think this ranch is worth?
PATRICE I have no idea.
MICHAEL Well, there are 20,000 acres at let's say $2,000 an acre *(He is counting zeroes on his fingers)* Wow, that's four million dollars No - wait a minute, that's forty million dollars
PATRICE It doesn't matter what it's worth, we can't sell it unless Jarvis agrees
MICHAEL That's right We'll have to find a way round that

(Enter JARVIS from the kitchen carrying a manila envelope and a large thermos bottle)

JARVIS Excuse me, please madam

PATRICE What is it Jarvis?

JARVIS *(Comes D C)* According to very specific instructions given to me by Mr Stancliffe before he died, immediately after the reading of the will, I was required to open his private safe, with the key he gave me, and bring its contents to you

PATRICE Oh What was in it?

JARVIS Just this thermos bottle and a sealed envelope with the words "Amazon Elixir Co" on the outside

MICHAEL Amazon Elixir Co? Of course Amelixco!

JARVIS Ah yes! I believe that would be it sir

MICHAEL Another mystery about to be revealed I must say the old boy certainly had a flair for the dramatic

JARVIS *(Tries to hand the envelope to PATRICE)* So, here you are madam

PATRICE No, no Don't you remember, you're the major shareholder, you open it

JARVIS Very well madam

PATRICE Why don't you sit down Jarvis?

JARVIS Thank you madam *(Sits on the L chair and opens the envelope)* Let me see now, there is something that looks like a list of ingredients and – ah, yes, a typewritten letter *(He turns it over)* There appears to be no signature *(He pauses, reading for a moment)*

MICHAEL Well? *(JARVIS continues to read)* Aren't you going to read it to us?

JARVIS Well, there's a long dissertation about how this formula is worth billions of dollars, about how dangerous it could be in the wrong hands, he mentions my experience and stability as reasons for making me the major shareholder, and *(He pauses)* Ah - Ah - ha!

MICHAEL What?

JARVIS I'm afraid sir, this appears to be another of Mr Stancliffe's, shall we say "eccentricities" sir?

PATRICE What do you mean?

JARVIS It states that this is a formula for, and a sample of, a love potion, madam

MICHAEL A love potion?

JARVIS A love potion sir
PATRICE That's ridiculous
MICHAEL I told you he was as nutty as a fruitcake
JARVIS In this instance sir, I am inclined to agree with you

(He continues to read)

PATRICE He can't have been that stupid I mean everyone knows there's no such thing as a love potion
JARVIS I absolutely agree with you madam, however there appears to be an interesting wrinkle to this love potion
PATRICE What do you mean?
JARVIS If I'm understanding this correctly, the potion does not claim to work on the person who drinks it
MICHAEL What?
JARVIS It claims that the potion causes the person who drinks it to give off some barely perceptible chemical odor, which it says affects the vomeronasal organ of the opposite sex, with devastating effect Here, you read it sir

(He hands the paper to MICHAEL)

PATRICE It's too stupid for words
JARVIS It is rather disappointing I agree I'm afraid we're just going to have to put this down to one of Mr Stancliffe's little jokes madam *(He stands)* I need to get organized for dinner this evening, so if you'll excuse me, I have work to do in the kitchen

(He exits to the kitchen)

MICHAEL *(Still reading)* Now that's kind of curious
PATRICE What is?
MICHAEL The key ingredient would appear to be a solution made by soaking the bark of the Imbuya tree in salt water
PATRICE What's an Imbuya tree?
MICHAEL I've no idea Wait a minute

(He gets up, goes up to the bookcase and takes out one of the encyclopedias)

PATRICE Michael, this is ridiculous There's no such thing as a love potion I know it, you know it, the whole world knows it
MICHAEL Here we are I-M-B-U-Y-A Brazilian walnut It's a common hard- wood tree from Amazonia

(He puts the book back then returns to the couch)

PATRICE Amazonia! That is curious What else does it say?
MICHAEL *(Reading the paper again)* That's about it It says the potion is fast acting and the effect doesn't last long
PATRICE Michael, stop You're beginning to sound like you believe this nonsense
MICHAEL *(Puts down the papers)* You're right, it's just too far fetched
PATRICE *(Gets up and heads for the stairs)* You know, everything happened so quickly I never finished unpacking Let me get that out of the way, and then we've got a lot to discuss Especially about Jarvis, and whether we're going to live here I'm not sure I like the idea of having him around permanently I won't be long

(She exits to the west wing MICHAEL watches her go, then picks up the thermos from the small table, unscrews the cap, looks inside, and smells the contents, as MELODY enters from the kitchen She crosses R picks up the second straight chair and heads to the kitchen as MICHAEL rushes to open the door for her She is about to go through it when she realizes her derriere is vulnerable to MICHAEL's hands She turns, and keeping the chair between herself and MICHAEL, exits to the kitchen MICHAEL looks wistfully after her, then is struck with a brilliant idea He goes back to the small table, picks up the thermos, looks at the kitchen door and takes a drink He then goes to the drinks table, pours something into a glass, then carefully drops it on the floor He tries to smell his own breath,

primps a little, then goes to the kitchen door and calls in)

MICHAEL I'm afraid I've spilled a drink Could you help me please Melody?

(He hurries back to the R of drinks table and waits MELODY enters from the kitchen with a cloth in her hand)

MICHAEL I'm sorry about this
MELODY That's alright sir To tell you the truth, I'm kind of glad someone else can do it as well as me *(She starts to bend down to mop up the spill, realizes she will have her back to Michael, turns and bends so she is facing him MICHAEL just stands there, expectantly leaning slightly towards her)* It won't take a minute What was it anyway?
MICHAEL Er - er - just water I think
MELODY Oh, that's easy then *(She completes the mopping and stands up)* There that does it

(MICHAEL stands still but leans closer to her She pauses for a second looking curiously at him, then turns and crosses L to the kitchen door MICHAEL smiles at her but remains standing just to the R of the drinks table MELODY pauses at the kitchen door, looks at him and exits to the kitchen MICHAEL shrugs There's is a momentary pause, then MELODY bursts through the kitchen door on the dead run She crosses R and flings herself at MICHAEL, smothering him with kisses Her momentum carries them both through the open center door MICHAEL staggers backwards across the bed MELODY rips off her skirt and flings it away, then leaps astride him on the bed, tearing at his clothes MICHAEL grabs her and they roll over on the bed He manages to get his jacket off, and MELODY undoes her blouse, as JARVIS, who has entered from the kitchen, appears in the center doorway)

JARVIS Trying to get the lay of the land are we sir? *(He picks up Melody's skirt and holds it out for her as they untangle themselves MELODY gets dressed)* If I may be so bold sir, perhaps it would be a good idea if you confined the activities of your baser instincts to your wife

MICHAEL No, no, you don't understand, it wasn't me

JARVIS Well, you could have fooled me!

MICHAEL No, no you see it all happened so quickly, it was just a -

JARVIS Tempest in a "D" cup sir? I shall for the moment remain silent about your conduct, but I cannot make the same guarantee should it happen again Come Melody

(MELODY and JARVIS exit to the kitchen MICHAEL follows them L , starts to protest, then shuts up and watches them go, as PATRICE enters from the west wing)

MICHAEL *(Rushes up to her)* It works

PATRICE What?

MICHAEL It works, the love potion, it works

PATRICE Baloney It's all in the head

MICHAEL *(Looks down)* That's not entirely true

PATRICE Nonsense

(She comes D and sits on the couch L end MICHAEL follows her down and sits on the couch R end)

MICHAEL Listen to me I drank some, and the maid, Melody, went berserk Her hormones were moving at warp speed

PATRICE What? Start again

MICHAEL I tried the love potion, and believe me, it works Melody couldn't keep her hands off me

PATRICE Baloney

MICHAEL Do you realize what this means? The implications are staggering Everyone on the planet will want to buy it Uncle Edward was right It's worth billions

PATRICE Michael, calm down I'm sure you're mistaken, and anyway why hasn't it affected me?

MICHAEL It's probably worn off The letter said it didn't last long

PATRICE Oh Michael, we both know what you're like I think you're believing it because you want to, why if everyone — *(She breaks off)* That's it, don't you see?
MICHAEL See what?
PATRICE You think it worked because you wanted it to
MICHAEL I'm not sure that was it at all I mean she really, you know, put a move on me I mean it I think it was the potion
PATRICE Of course you do, and that's the point This is the answer to our problem with Jarvis
MICHAEL Now you've really lost me
PATRICE Don't you see? If we could convince Jarvis the love potion works, he'd give us anything for our 50% of the shares
MICHAEL You mean "anything" as in his rights to the ranch
PATRICE Precisely
MICHAEL How do you propose to do that?
PATRICE We'll have to plan very carefully The first thing we're going to have to do is get him to drink some of the stuff Then, I guess it'll have to be up to me to convince him it works
MICHAEL You and Jarvis That's ridiculous
PATRICE The more unlikely it seems, the more he's liable to believe it Sh!

(Enter JARVIS from the kitchen, he comes D to the front door)

JARVIS Excuse me madam I believe a car has just pulled up

(He opens the front door It is still raining Enter TAMMY-JO and OAKFIELD They are still in their rain gear, but absolutely drenched PATRICE and MICHAEL are on their feet JARVIS closes the front door)

PATRICE Good heavens, you're absolutely soaked What happened?
T-JO Mr Oakfield's car got stuck on the creek bridge The flood level was over two feet when I got there He shouldn't have tried to cross

JARVIS Give me your coats everyone *(They hand JARVIS their wet raincoats We see the lower part of Oakfield's pants and TAMMY-JO's skirt are wet)* Are you alright sir?

OAKFIELD I'm fine Really I am

T-JO I've seen a lot of flash floods here, but this one came up real fast

(JARVIS takes the coats and exits to the kitchen)

PATRICE Here, sit down for a minute I'll get you both a little brandy

(She goes to the drinks table as TAMMY-JO and OAKFIELD sit on the couch)

T-JO Well, one thing's for sure, we're not going to cross the creek today

MICHAEL You mean you'll have to stay here?

T-JO I'm sorry to impose on you, but we really don't have any alternative It'll take several hours for the creek to go down, even if it stopped raining right now, which it doesn't look like it's going to do

(JARVIS returns from the kitchen followed by MELODY)

JARVIS Melody, there are some large towels in the powder room in the study *(MELODY crosses R into the study and exits to the powder room)* She won't be a second

(PATRICE comes D L with two brandy glasses which she hands to OAKFIELD and TAMMY-JO)

PATRICE Jarvis, Miss Harper was just telling us that both she and Mr Oakfield will have to stay here tonight Can you manage all that?

JARVIS Of course madam These two rooms *(He steps up to the landing and indicates B R 1 and B R 2)* are more than adequate You will however have to share the bathroom in the middle

(MELODY enters from the powder room with towels, which she hands to TAMMYY-JO and OAKFIELD)

PATRICE You'll need some dry clothes and I'm afraid I only brought one small suitcase
MELODY I could try to find something if you like
T-JO That would be real nice Thank you
JARVIS I think perhaps I could try to find something for you Mr Oakfield Why don't you come with me sir?

(OAKFIELD, MELODY and TAMMY-JO all head towards the west wing)

OAKFIELD Thank you
MELODY I'm not sure we really wear the same kind of clothes, but I'll let you see what I've got
T-JO Don't worry, anything will do

(MELODY, TAMMY-JO, OAKFIELD and JARVIS all exit to the west wing PATRICE pauses at the foot of the stairs, watches them go, then turns to Michael)

PATRICE Perfect!
MICHAEL What's perfect?
PATRICE Well, now Miss Harper is here, maybe she could help us convince Jarvis that the love potion works
MICHAEL Why in heaven's name would she do that?
PATRICE Easy! What makes the world go round? We'll pay her to do it

(She sits on the sofa, picks up her purse from the coffee table, takes out a pen and check book and writes)

MICHAEL That's not going to work You're never going to get

Jarvis to drink that stuff

PATRICE Hmm! You're probably right We're going to have to slip it to him and tell him afterwards Michael, would you open a bottle of wine please and pour one glass

MICHAEL What are you going to do?

(He goes to the drinks table, finds a corkscrew and opens a bottle of wine)

PATRICE We'll ask Jarvis to try this wine Then we'll pay Miss Harper to put a move on him, and later we'll tell him he drank some of the potion That way he'll believe it works

MICHAEL *(Holds up the thermos)* Should I really put some in?

PATRICE Why not? It'll be a reason for the wine to taste funny

MICHAEL *(Pouring a little from the thermos into the glass of wine)* Did I ever tell you, you have a devious mind?

(Enter TAMMY-JO and MELODY from the west wing TAMMY-JO carries a bundle of clothes)

T-JO This is real nice of you Thanks

MELODY You're welcome, I just hope everything fits

(She comes straight down and exits to the kitchen)

T-JO *(Hesitates on the landing)* Which of these rooms should I take?

PATRICE *(Gets up and goes to the foot of the stairs)* I don't suppose it matters, but before you change, could I have a word with you please?

T-JO Sure Why not

(She drapes the clothes over the landing rail, and comes down)

PATRICE Please sit down for a minute

T-JO Okay *(Sits L chair)*

PATRICE *(Sits couch R end)* You're going to think this a little strange, but I wonder if you would cooperate with us in playing a little joke on Jarvis

T-JO What sort of joke?

PATRICE We'd like you to - er - sort of - er - make a pass at him

T-JO Jarvis! Why?

MICHAEL *(Comes D to the R of the R chair)* Well, he's such a stuffy old thing We thought it might be kind of amusing

T-JO If you don't mind my saying so Mr Leadley, I don't think that's in very good taste

PATRICE I was afraid you might say that Here, *(She hands her the check)* perhaps this check might persuade you

T-JO Five thousand dollars! *(She looks at both of them)* Just exactly what is it you want me to do?

PATRICE Well, we'd like you to - er - I'm not too sure how to put this Could you, just for a short while, er - act as though he was absolutely irresistible to you?

T-JO Jarvis? You want me to come on to him?

PATRICE Well yes, but just for five minutes

T-JO Five minutes? You're going to pay me five thousand dollars for five minutes?

PATRICE Well, almost We may have to call on you later for a repeat performance Ten minutes at the most

T-JO You're on! You're crazy, but you're on

PATRICE Can you do it? Can you convince him?

T-JO Piece of cake! Men are all easy!

MICHAEL What do you mean, men are all easy?

T-JO Well, when you unzip their pants their brains fall out

MICHAEL That's not fair

T-JO Listen, women may want a reason to have sex, but men just need a place Anyway, don't tell me men have never used sex to get what they want

MICHAEL How can we possibly use sex to get what we want Sex is what we want

PATRICE Michael!

T-JO *(Stands)* Let me get changed and I'll get right to it

(She goes up to the landing Enter JARVIS and OAKFIELD from the west wing OAKFIELD is wearing a robe and JARVIS is carrying OAKFIELD's pants)

JARVIS Ah, Miss Harper, why don't you take this room

(He opens the door of B R 2)

T-JO Thank you Jarvis

(She picks up the clothes from the railing and exits to B R 2 JARVIS continues R to B R 1)

JARVIS You should be quite comfortable in here sir *(Opens the door of B R 1)* I'm sorry I didn't have much to fit you, but I'll have your pants dried and pressed in no time
OAKFIELD Thank you Jarvis

(OAKFIELD exits B R 1 JARVIS comes down and heads towards the kitchen)

PATRICE Jarvis

(She moves to the drinks table)

JARVIS *(By the kitchen door)* Yes madam?
PATRICE We just opened this wine, and it tastes a little strange to me Do you think you could taste it please?
JARVIS With pleasure madam *(He crosses R and takes the proffered glass He holds it up to the light, smells it, twirls it around, looks at it and finally takes the tiniest sip)* You're right madam, it is a little odd I can't quite put my finger on it *(Takes another sip)* Strange
MICHAEL Perhaps if you took a big gulp it might help
JARVIS We do not gulp wine sir However, *(He takes a good mouthful)* there is nothing wrong with the wine madam, it simply

has no body, no fruit, no texture, almost as though it had been watered down May I see the bottle? *(Patrice hands him the bottle)* Very odd I would have expected more from that *(Takes one more drink)* Very disappointing

PATRICE Oh well, never mind Now, Michael and I are going to help you in the kitchen

JARVIS I'm quite sure Melody and I can manage madam

PATRICE No, we insist, after all, we've got to prepare dinner for — good heavens, it's six people now Come along Michael

(PATRICE and MICHAEL exit to the kitchen JARVIS holds up the glass of wine and looks at it He then picks up the thermos and looks in it trying to see the liquid level, pauses, looks at the kitchen door, then looks again at the thermos Enter TAMMY-JO from B R 2 She has not changed but is carrying a dry outfit She opens the bathroom door)

JARVIS Have you got everything you need miss?

T-JO Well, I really could use a couple more towels

JARVIS Right away miss *(Goes to the kitchen door and holds it open)* Melody!

T-JO *(In the doorway of the bathroom)* Jarvis, do you ever have any fun?

JARVIS I beg your pardon miss? *(MELODY enters from the kitchen)* Ah Melody, could you please get Miss Harper some more towels, and then we'll need to dry and press Mr Oakfield's pants *(He hands her the pants)*

MELODY Sure Back in a jiffy

(She exits to west wing, carrying the pants T-JO drapes the clothes over the railing and comes down to JARVIS)

T-JO What I meant was, what do you do for recreation? You know fun?

JARVIS Well miss, I enjoy reading Shakespeare, playing chess, crossword puzzles -

T-JO Whoopee!

JARVIS That too miss

T-JO Why Jarvis! *(Now very close to him, almost chest to chest)* Would you like to have dinner some night?

JARVIS I like to have dinner every night miss

T-JO Has anyone ever told you you're a very attractive man?

JARVIS Thank you Miss Harper That's very kind of you to say so, but you really should get out of those wet clothes

T-JO What a good idea

(She starts to unbutton her shirt and advances on him till he is up against the kitchen door JARVIS ducks across in front of her and escapes R)

JARVIS Oh my goodness, that's not what I meant

T-JO *(Continues her pursuit as JARVIS backs away R)* You know I never noticed your eyes before

JARVIS My eyes?

T-JO Your eyes, *(She runs her fingers all over him, his hair, behind his ears, down his chest, etc JARVIS continues to back away R his eyes never leave her fingers as he reacts to every move)* your hair, your neck, your chest, your arms

(She grabs him and gives him a big passionate kiss)

JARVIS Oh my goodness *(He looks around, but the only escape is through the center door TAMMY-JO follows, sees the bed, very deliberately closes the center door behind her, and continues her advance)* Miss Harper I really think you should try to control yourself

T-JO Why? Don't you find me attractive?

JARVIS Indeed I have always found you attractive Miss Harper, but this is hardly the time and place

(PATRICE and MICHAEL enter from the kitchen, tip-toe across to the center door and listen)

T-JO I don't know about the time, but for the life of me I can't think of a better place

JARVIS *(Backing down toward the bed and looking at it over his shoulder)* Really Miss Harper, I don't think this is a good idea at all What's Mrs Leadley going to say?

T-JO I don't care what anybody says, I just want you, you great big beautiful butler

(JARVIS is now trapped above the bed with no place left to go TAMMY-JO pushes him down on the bed and flings herself on top of him smothering him with kisses)

PATRICE She really seems to be putting on a very convincing show

MICHAEL Sh! Come on We don't want to be caught out here We can watch from the kitchen

(They return to the kitchen, but can just be seen peeking out from behind the slightly ajar door)

JARVIS *(Struggles free)* Miss Harper, that's enough, please control yourself

T-JO. *(Sits up and straightens her clothes)* It's difficult, but I'll try

(JARVIS escapes back into the living room)

JARVIS We really must try to maintain some sense of decorum Now please go and change your clothes

(TAMMY-JO follows him into the living room and moves L to the stairs as JARVIS backs away)

T-JO O K. But I'm not finished I'm definitely going to see you later

(She goes up stairs)

JARVIS Oh dear!

(Enter MELODY from the west wing with two large towels)

MELODY Here you are miss

(TAMMY-JO takes the towels, picks up the clothes from the railing and exits to the bathroom, closing the door)

T-JO Thanks
JARVIS Thank you Melody
MELODY You're welcome

(She comes down and, as she gets close to JARVIS, she stops, takes a deep breath, looks around then gives him a long lingering kiss, watched by PATRICE and MICHAEL from the kitchen door Then, without saying a word, she exits to the west wing JARVIS looks puzzled, watches her go, then heads R towards the center door He stops by the drinks table, picks up the thermos, looks towards the west wing, puts down the thermos, then goes into the study and straightens out the bedcovers, as PATRICE and MICHAEL enter from the kitchen)

PATRICE *(Crosses R to the center door)* Ah, there you are Jarvis Could we see you for a moment please?

(JARVIS enters the living room)

JARVIS Of course madam
PATRICE There's something we need to tell you *(She pauses JARVIS just stands there offering no help)* Would you like a seat? *(JARVIS reacts)* I mean, would you like to sit down?
JARVIS Very well madam

(He sits on the L chair, MICHAEL and PATRICE sit on the couch)

PATRICE I'm afraid we have a confession to make
JARVIS Confession madam?

PATRICE Yes I know it's silly, and of course there's no such
thing as a love potion, but Mr Leadley got this idea it might work,
and insisted we test it

JARVIS Test it madam?

PATRICE Yes So we - er - oh this is so embarrassing Michael,
you tell him

MICHAEL Well, we - er - we put some in that wine you drank

JARVIS Really sir, I must protest If you wanted to test it, why
not drink it yourselves?

MICHAEL Well, we thought of that, and then we thought it
would be better if the person drinking it didn't know

PATRICE I think we got a little carried away with the idea it
might work We really do apologize Jarvis What we did was very
foolish and we are sorry

JARVIS I see Well, there's no harm done I suppose, and yet I
can't help wondering   *(He trails off, frowning and looking very
thoughtful, then goes up to the drinks table, picks up the wine glass
and looks at it)*

MICHAEL *(After a slight pause)* Well, what is it?

JARVIS Well, Miss Harper, she - er - *(He looks through the
study door)* no, no, it's ridiculous

MICHAEL What's ridiculous?

JARVIS Well, she - er *(He looks at the bathroom door)* it's just
too fantastic It's no matter sir I must get back to the kitchen

*(He exits to the kitchen PATRICE gets up and follows him almost to
the kitchen door, then stands looking at it)*

PATRICE Did you see that? We've sown the seed of doubt He's
starting to believe the love potion works Now the next step to really
convince him is to find a way to do it again later

MICHAEL You didn't notice did you?

PATRICE. Notice what?

MICHAEL Melody

PATRICE What about Melody?

MICHAEL She kissed him, and you didn't pay her Maybe it

really does work

PATRICE Michael, please don't start that again

MICHAEL Then how do you explain it?

PATRICE It's Melody, she's a flake, you've seen her, she probably kisses everybody

MICHAEL Oh, I never thought of that *(Pause)* She never kissed me!

PATRICE Of course not, she's an employee, she wouldn't kiss you Now, you need to go and unpack your things I've done all mine

MICHAEL *(Heads upstairs)* O K But I'm not convinced I think we should definitely run some more tests

PATRICE Yes, you'd like that wouldn't you, with you as the chief guinea-pig no doubt Go and unpack Michael

(MICHAEL exits to the west wing There is a pounding on the front door PATRICE crosses D L and opens it Enter MARY-LOU Age perhaps 30-40, she is wearing a huge waterproof poncho and rain hat, and carrying a large carry-all She steps into the room We see it is still raining PATRICE closes the door)

M-LOU Hello I'm Mary-Lou Winston Is Jarvis here please?

PATRICE Yes, of course, I'll get him.

(She goes to the kitchen door)

M-LOU I'm sorry to burst in like this I didn't know Jarvis had company

PATRICE *(Calls in the kitchen door)* Jarvis *(Comes back down)* Would you like to take your poncho off?

(JARVIS enters from the kitchen and comes D)

JARVIS Good heavens, Miss Winston What are you doing here? Here, let me help you

(He takes the poncho and hat MARY-LOU is revealed She is a

severe looking woman Her hair is up in a bun, she wears plain
wire rimmed glasses and no make-up She is wearing blue jeans
and a denim shirt She has on a small back-pack which she takes
off after the poncho)

JARVIS Mrs Leadley, may I introduce you to Mary-Lou
Winston Mrs Leadley is Mr Stancliffe's niece and the new owner of
the L P Circle Ranch
M-LOU How do you do *(They shake hands)*
PATRICE Hello
JARVIS Miss Winston is engaged in a woodpecker preservation
program out in the North section
M-LOU Actually I'm doing research for my masters in ornithology
JARVIS You're shivering my dear Are you alright?
PATRICE I'll get you a little brandy

(She goes to the drinks table)

M-LOU Thank you
JARVIS What brings you to the house?
M-LOU Well, you know where I have my campsite?
JARVIS Yes, of course
M-LOU Well, it's a sea of mud I mean it's just awful, and I
wondered if I could spend the night here?
PATRICE *(Comes D and hands her the brandy)* Well Jarvis,
what do you say? What's one more?
JARVIS Well, we've finally run out of bedrooms madam We
could give her the study or she could share with Miss Harper
M-LOU Oh I don't mind sharing at all
JARVIS Well, that's probably best, the study is a little spartan

(Enter TAMMY-JO from the bathroom She is now wearing a knee
length skirt and blouse and no shoes She carries her original
skirt, blouse and boots She comes down the steps)

T-JO Oh hi Mary-Lou What brings you here?

M-LOU I got rained out I've never seen anything like it

JARVIS Miss Harper, do you suppose you could share your room with Miss Winston?

T-JO Sure, it'll be fun Could I please put these things somewhere to dry?

JARVIS Of course, give them to me I'll take care of them

(He starts to take them from TAMMY-JO, but as he is already holding MARY-LOU's poncho and hat, has some difficulty)

PATRICE Here, I'll give you a hand

(She takes some of the clothes)

JARVIS Thank you madam

(JARVIS and PATRICE exit to the kitchen)

M-LOU Why are you staying here?

T-JO The creek bridge is out, so I'm here till tomorrow at least

M-LOU Did I hear Jarvis say Mr Stancliffe left the ranch to Mrs Leadley?

T-JO That's right

M-LOU He must be disappointed

T-JO Oh I'm sure But I think he half expected it, and you know Jarvis, he won't let it upset him Anyway, *(She heads up)* you finish your drink I'd better straighten our room up I've only been here half an hour and it's a mess already

(She exits to B R 2 Left alone on stage, MARY-LOU sits on the couch and sips her brandy She pulls a face and goes up to the drinks table She pours some "water" from the love potion thermos into her glass She stands at the drinks table and takes a sip Her facial expression indicates it tastes better She returns to the couch and drains her glass as MICHAEL enters from the west wing)

MICHAEL Oh, hello
M-LOU Hello
MICHAEL *(Comes D to shake her hand)* I'm Michael Leadley
M-LOU *(Stands)* I'm Mary-Lou Winston I'm pleased to meet you

(She offers her hand He takes her hand, kisses it, pauses, looks at her, and smells it)

MICHAEL Not nearly as pleased as I am to meet you

(He stands staring at her)

M-LOU What?
MICHAEL Here, please sit down
M-LOU Thank you

(She sits on the couch just left of center MICHAEL sits beside her on the couch R end)

MICHAEL You know I suddenly find you very attractive
M-LOU Me?
MICHAEL *(Puts his left arm around her)* Oh, yes Don't you feel it?
M-LOU *(Inching away L on the couch)* Feel what?
MICHAEL *(Moving L close to her again)* It's like a rising tide of passion. swelling up inside, ready to burst out like an exploding super-nova
M-LOU *(Now at the extreme L end of the couch)* Good heavens, do you always say things like that to perfect strangers?
MICHAEL *(Gazing into her eyes)* Yes, yes, you are
M-LOU Yes, I'm what?
MICHAEL Perfect!

(He moves to put his right arm around her, but she ducks out of his grasp and stands up)

M-LOU But I'm a Presbyterian!

MICHAEL Well, alright then, almost perfect!

(He gets up MARY-LOU escapes D S of the coffee table and then crosses R)

M-LOU Mr Leadley, I want to assure you that I am not the sort of woman you can play fast and loose with

(MICHAEL approaches her D R , as she escapes U C behind the chairs)

MICHAEL Ah, but you do want to play huh?

(He follows her)

M-LOU *(Backing L towards the couch)* If you don't stop I shall do something desperate
MICHAEL That sounds exciting, tell me more
M-LOU Don't you ever give up?
MICHAEL No It's in my genes
M-LOU Yes, and that's where it's going to stay

(He lunges for her She falls backwards over the R arm of the couch MICHAEL falls on top of her as JARVIS enters from the kitchen)

JARVIS Feeling right on top of things now, are we sir?

(MARY-LOU extricates herself and rushes U.C to JARVIS)

M-LOU Mr Jarvis This — this beast — he tried to — to put his hand on me

(PATRICE enters from the kitchen)

PATRICE Michael, what going on here?
MICHAEL *(Gets up, looking rather sheepish)* I don't know

what came over me

M-LOU Well I do Your hormones are hanging out all over the place

PATRICE I think I need to have a word with you In private Michael

JARVIS Ahem! Let me show you to your room miss *(He picks up MARY-LOU's hold-all and heads up the stairs, followed by MARY-LOU, who picks up her back-pack JARVIS knocks on the door of B R 2, which is opened by TAMMY-JO)* May we come in miss?

T-JO Of course

(She turns back into the room)

JARVIS Thank you

(He goes into B R 2)

MICHAEL Miss Winston *(MARY-LOU stops in the doorway of B R 2 and turns D S MICHAEL has come up to the drinks table and holds up the thermos)* I'm really sorry about my behavior, but did you by any chance drink any of this?

M-LOU What that has to do with your lascivious behavior I can't imagine, but yes, I did

(She exits to B R 2, leaving the door open)

MICHAEL That's it! That's it! The love potion, it works, don't you see?

(JARVIS comes out of B R 2, closes the door behind him, comes down, gives MICHAEL a withering look and exits to the kitchen)

PATRICE Michael, if you're going to use that as an excuse, that's pathetic

MICHAEL I'm telling you it works I couldn't help myself

PATRICE You never can You've been doing this for years

MICHAEL But this was different Please believe me At least listen

(PATRICE comes D L and sits on the couch)

PATRICE Alright, tell me what happened
MICHAEL *(Pacing a little behind the chairs)* Well, I came into the room and she was there, so I introduced myself, shook hands with her and —
PATRICE You touched her?
MICHAEL I told you, we shook hands
PATRICE Did you smell her?
MICHAEL Well, not consciously, but I was standing right next to her
PATRICE Yes I'll bet you were
MICHAEL What do I have to do to convince you it works?
PATRICE Alright Michael I'll tell you what we'll do I still think you're up to your old tricks again, but I'll give you the benefit of the doubt We'll do a test, but this time we'll do it properly
MICHAEL Alright How?
PATRICE Let me think
MICHAEL Why not let me drink it this time?
PATRICE Oh you'd love that wouldn't you No, not you You'd expect it to work, and not Jarvis either I know, we'll give some to Mr Oakfield

*(MELODY has entered from the west wing **[See AUTHOR'S NOTE]** She is carrying MR OAKFIELD's pants over her arm She goes up to B R 1 and knocks PATRICE puts her finger to her lips, signaling to MICHAEL to say nothing OAKFIELD opens the door)*

MELODY Here you are sir
OAKFIELD Thank you Melody

(OAKFIELD exits to B R 1 MELODY exits to the west wing looking strangely at MICHAEL and PATRICE, who just smile at her)

MICHAEL I'll tell you what, if any of the women in this house
go for Oakfield, we'll know for sure it works
PATRICE What do you mean?
MICHAEL Well, he's not exactly Robert Redford, is he?
PATRICE Oh I don't know I think he has a certain charm
MICHAEL He's about as charming as a sewage treatment plant
PATRICE Michael!

(She gets up)

MICHAEL Well, I suppose there's no accounting for taste
PATRICE *(Now at the drinks table)* Now, the first thing to do
is to pour this stuff into the water jug *(She pours the love potion out
of the thermos into the empty water jug)* Michael fill this up with
water please

(She hands him the thermos)

MICHAEL O K

(He exits to kitchen)

PATRICE I'll just get Mr Oakfield

(She goes up to B R 1 and knocks)

OAKFIELD *(Off)* Come in

*(PATRICE exits to B R 1 and closes the door MELODY enters from
the west wing with a vacuum cleaner She carries the vacuum
cleaner in her right hand and the power cord, coiled rather
untidily, in her left She comes down and, as she turns left to go
towards the kitchen, a loop of the cord catches on the newel
post She turns to try to untangle it, but only succeeds in
wrapping the cord around herself She twists and turns but only
makes matters worse Her skirt rides up as she tries to extricate*

herself MICHAEL enters from the kitchen with the thermos, he rushes over to the drinks table, puts it down and turns to help MELODY)

MICHAEL Here, let me help
(His hands are all over her as JARVIS enters from the kitchen)

JARVIS Trying not to lose touch are we sir?

(At this point in their struggles MELODY manages to bring her knee up striking MICHAEL in the crotch He gives a piercing yell and collapses on the ground at the foot of the stairs holding his crotch Both bedroom doors open PATRICE, followed by OAKFIELD, now no longer in his robe, but wearing his pants again, comes out of B R 1 TAMMY-JO steps out of B R 2 MARY-LOU is behind her hastily putting on a robe MELODY is still on the steps totally entangled by the vacuum cord)

PATRICE What happened?
JARVIS I believe Mr Leadley finally got a hold of himself, but there's no cause for alarm madam Miss Melody seems to have her wires crossed and as for your husband, you'll have to forgive him, he's still feeling his way around
MICHAEL O-o-o-a-a-r-g-h-!
PATRICE I'll just bet he is

(JARVIS helps MELODY up and untangles her)

JARVIS Come along Melody We'll do the vacuuming later Why don't you help me with dinner?

(JARVIS and MELODY exit to the kitchen TAMMY-JO and MARY-LOU return to B R 2 and close the door MICHAEL, still groaning, slumps onto the couch, R end PATRICE comes down to the drinks table, followed by OAKFIELD who sits on the L chair.)

PATRICE Let me get you that drink Mr Oakfield Did you say scotch and water?

OAKFIELD Yes, thank you Are you alright?

MICHAEL I'll be O K in a minute *(PATRICE has poured a small scotch and now adds "water" from the love potion jug which she holds up for MICHAEL to see)* You know I'm going to stay well away from that girl

OAKFIELD You mean the maid, Melody?

MICHAEL Darn right I mean the maid She's a disaster area

(PATRICE comes D and hands the drink to OAKFIELD)

PATRICE Here you are.

OAKFIELD Thank you *(He drinks)* You know that's just what the doctor ordered *(Drinks again)*

PATRICE Michael, perhaps you should go and get ready for dinner while Mr Oakfield has his drink

MICHAEL I thought I'd keep him company and have one with him

PATRICE Oh I'm sure the other ladies *(She emphasizes the word, pauses and looks at MICHAEL)* will be here soon, and Mr Oakfield will have plenty of company

MICHAEL Oh yes I see what you mean *(He gets up very gingerly, his hands still clutching his crotch)* I think I might lie down before dinner anyway

(He exits to the west wing)

PATRICE I'll be there in a minute *(She follows MICHAEL U S a little, waits till he is out of sight, then comes down behind and slightly to the left of OAKFIELD's chair)* How's your drink?

OAKFIELD Just fine thank you *(Drinks again)*

PATRICE *(Leaning over him)* You know, if you don't mind my saying so you do smell absolutely delicious

OAKFIELD I think you're letting your imagination run away with you

PATRICE *(Leans closer)* No really

OAKFIELD Well, thank you I really don't know what to say

PATRICE *(Her eyes closed as she breathes in deeply)* They say actions speak louder than words

OAKFIELD Well, this is hardly the time or the place Suppose someone were to come in

PATRICE Meaning my husband I suppose?

OAKFIELD Yes Meaning your husband

PATRICE Alright then, come on!

(She takes hold of his hands, pulls him up, then pulls him with her into the study Closing the door, she leads him down to the bed)

OAKFIELD You know, I'm not sure this is really very sensible

PATRICE Oh come on, loosen up a bit

(She tickles him and they fall over together on the bed She continues to tickle him and attempts to kiss him)

OAKFIELD Oh my goodness me — oh — oh — oh

(He yells and laughs as she continues to tickle him, and they roll over and over on the bed JARVIS, hearing the noise, enters from the kitchen, crosses R , opens the study door and stands there)

JARVIS *(Eventually)* I see you have an interest in legal briefs madam!

PATRICE *(Gets up)* Oh my goodness This is amazing

JARVIS I must admit I find it somewhat incredible myself

OAKFIELD *(Gets up)* I don't know what got into us

PATRICE But I do, or, to be more precise, I know what got into you

OAKFIELD I can assure you Mrs Leadley that it was you, not I who —

PATRICE Of course it was me, but that was because you drank

some of the love potion
  OAKFIELD What?

(PATRICE crosses L past JARVIS through the center door to the drinks table, JARVIS follows with OAKFIELD close behind him)

PATRICE The water in your scotch and water I must have, sort of, accidentally poured it out of the wrong jug I forgot we'd put the love potion in the water jug, and water in the thermos

(She shows them the thermos and the nearly full water jug)

  JARVIS. Sort of, accidentally madam?
  PATRICE Yes
  JARVIS Forgot?
  PATRICE Yes, but that doesn't matter, what's important is that it seems to work. *(Crosses R in front of JARVIS and leans close to OAKFIELD)* As a matter of fact, it's still working *(Moves her lips towards his)*
  JARVIS *(Gently pulls her away)* Perhaps coffee in the kitchen might be a good idea madam
  PATRICE *(Gazing into OAKFIELD's eyes)* Do I have to?
  JARVIS *(Leads her gently L)* Yes indeed madam
  PATRICE Oh Alright Thank you Jarvis
  JARVIS Excuse us sir. *(MELODY enters from the kitchen)* Ah Melody, perhaps you'd like to get Mr Oakfield another drink while I get some coffee for Mrs Leadley It's a scotch and water I think, but let's make sure we don't make the same mistake again, so please use the water in the thermos not the water jug
  MELODY You want me to pour the drink?
  JARVIS You can do it *(Picks up OAKFIELD's glass from the table)* Was this it?
  OAKFIELD Yes
  JARVIS *(Smells it)* Right I think I'd better get rid of this Now, how about that coffee?

(JARVIS, carrying the glass, and PATRICE exit to the kitchen OAKFIELD sits in the L chair while MELODY mixes his drink She pours the water from the thermos)

OAKFIELD Is Jarvis always like that?

MELODY Like what?

OAKFIELD Well, you know, always in control, nothing seems to faze him

MELODY I suppose so, but he's really very sweet once you get to know him

OAKFIELD How long has he been here?

MELODY Ever since Mr Stancliffe bought the ranch, about thirty years ago Your drink's all ready

OAKFIELD Thank you *(He waits expectantly)*

MELODY Would you mind if I didn't hand it to you?

OAKFIELD Not at all

(He gets up and goes to the drinks table, passing very close to MELODY who closes her eyes and breathes in deeply He picks up the drink and returns to his chair)

MELODY Thank you

(She comes down behind him, and leans over, breathing deeply during the following speech MELODY starts to touch him First, just a finger on his shoulder, then her fingers run down his arm a little, then the other arm, then the back of her hand lightly across his cheek Then a finger through his hair, then his ears, neck, etc OAKFIELD sits absolutely motionless, his body frozen The only part of his body that moves are his eyeballs, growing ever larger as they follow the fingers up, down, and around)

MELODY You know Mr Oakfield, everyone thinks just because I drop things, that I'm some kind of air-head But they're all wrong I'm really a very deep thinker I've decided the reason men and

women don't understand each other is because they're different sexes
Except Jarvis I mean he is a different sex but he understands me He
appreciates me for what I am He makes me watch some of those
public television programs You know, the ones that start in the
middle, end at the beginning and you never know what's happened
Jarvis says they're educational We watch them a lot, especially after
Mr Stancliffe died and we didn't have anything to do Well, not
much anyway, and do you know what I got to thinking about? Well,
if you do nothing, how do you know when you're finished?

(OAKFIELD gets up and escapes D L near the front door)

    OAKFIELD That's very interesting I'm sure, but don't you have
something you ought to be doing now?
    MELODY *(Following him D L)* Are you married?
    OAKFIELD What?
    MELODY *(Now has him trapped against the front door and is
running her fingers up and down his chest)* What I mean is, are you,
you know, available?
    OAKFIELD Oh my dear lord!

*(He looks around for any avenue of escape, then suddenly runs R in
front of the chairs)*

    MELODY Because if you are, I want you
    OAKFIELD Really miss, I don't know what's got into you

*(MELODY follows him R , flings her arms around his neck and
attempts to kiss him)*

    MELODY Neither do I, and I really don't care.

*(OAKFIELD ducks out from under her arms, and momentarily
escapes U S close to the study door)*

    OAKFIELD Miss Melody, I absolutely insist that you stop this immediately

MELODY *(Flings herself at him)* What do you mean stop? We haven't started yet

OAKFIELD Started what? *(Realizes this is a stupid question)* Oh no!

(He runs into the study)

MELODY Oh yes!

(She follows him into the study He backs away toward the bed)

OAKFIELD Oh no

MELODY *(She now has him trapped above the bed)* Oh yes!

OAKFIELD But it's five o'clock in the afternoon

(He falls backwards across the bed MELODY hitches her skirt way, way up and kneels astride him on the bed)

MELODY What's wrong with love in the afternoon?

(PATRICE has entered from the kitchen and crossed R to the study door)

PATRICE What's wrong with it is that there are people wandering around and you usually get caught!

(OAKFIELD breaks away and rushes up to PATRICE just inside the study door)

OAKFIELD Thank goodness you're here

PATRICE *(To MELODY who gets off the bed and straightens her clothing)* I think perhaps you ought to confine your afternoon activities to the kitchen Melody

MELODY Yes ma'am

(She crosses L and exits to the kitchen)

OAKFIELD My dear —

(PATRICE puts her finger to his lips They wait till MELODY has entered the kitchen then PATRICE closes the study door)

PATRICE Pookie!
OAKFIELD Snookums!

(They kiss passionately)

PATRICE I was mad with jealousy when I saw you with the maid
OAKFIELD Whatever made her behave like that?
PATRICE She seems to be like that all the time
OAKFIELD Oh Snookums, I can't go on much longer just loving you on Thursdays I want you all the time We can't go on meeting behind his back You must divorce him
PATRICE Oh Pookie, I will I will Don't you see it's all working It's just as I explained it to you They're all starting to believe the love potion works Once we get them totally convinced Michael will take half my shares in Amelixco as his part of the divorce settlement and we'll be free of him Jarvis will take the other half and give up his rights to the ranch and everything will be ours
OAKFIELD Oh Snookums!
PATRICE Oh Pookie!

(They kiss passionately as —)

THE CURTAIN FALLS

.

ACT II

(Later the same evening After dinner The coffee cups, glasses, etc have been cleared away It is now dark outside and has stopped raining)

(The curtain rises on an empty set Immediately MELODY enters from the kitchen and holds the door open for JARVIS who enters carrying a tray with coffee, cups, etc He is followed by PATRICE, MICHAEL and OAKFIELD JARVIS comes D and puts the tray on the coffee table)

JARVIS Here you are madam
PATRICE Thank you Jarvis

(PATRICE and OAKFILED sit on the couch MICHAEL remains standing U R ogling MELODY who stays U L)

JARVIS It finally seems to have stopped raining, so while Miss Harper and Miss Winston are out looking at the creek bridge, I think I'll just go and open a few windows in the bedrooms It's really got quite stuffy in here
MELODY I can do that
JARVIS *(Hesitates)* Well, *(MELODY looks imploringly at him)* O K Thank you
(MELODY goes up and into B R 1 leaving the door open MICHAEL watches her go)

PATRICE Well Jarvis, I think we ought to congratulate you on an excellent dinner

(She pours coffee)

JARVIS I think we can all congratulate each other madam, it really was a team effort

OAKFIELD You know I quite enjoyed it It's not very often I get into a kitchen

(There is an enormous thump from B R 1)

MICHAEL *(Rushes up and into B R 1)* Here, let me help

(JARVIS follows him up and waits expectantly outside the door of B R 1 There is a scream from MELODY, followed by a huge thud, followed by a groan of pain from MICHAEL Everyone turns U S to watch as MELODY comes out of B R 1 smiles at everyone and goes into B R 2 leaving the door open MICHAEL reappears bent over in pain, holding his crotch, his face contorted in agony)

JARVIS Still hanging in there are we sir?

MICHAEL I think I'll skip coffee and go and lie down for a few minutes

(Still doubled over, MICHAEL limps off to the west wing There is yet another series of thumps and crashes from B R 2 They all look up expectantly as MELODY appears from B R 2 and closes the door behind her)

MELODY *(Smiling proudly)* There, that's fixed that window

JARVIS *(Goes L to MELODY)* I think perhaps I'll help you with the other windows Melody Excuse me madam

(JARVIS and MELODY exit to the west wing PATRICE and OAKFIELD watch them go, then turn towards each other)

PATRICE Pookie!

OAKFIELD Snookums! *(They embrace)* Alone at last *(They kiss)*

PATRICE *(Breaking away and looking around)* We must be careful, if we're caught together, we won't be able to blame the love potion again

OAKFIELD I know, but you did a fabulous job of pretending it worked

PATRICE It wasn't very hard you know

OAKFIELD I meant what I said I can't take much more of this sneaking around Thursday afternoons are not enough

PATRICE I know, but it won't be long now We just have to get Jarvis totally convinced the love potion works, and then we'll make him an offer he can't refuse

OAKFIELD And your husband?

PATRICE I think he's convinced already, and anyway with Michael it's not just the money he thinks the love potion will make He probably imagines himself drinking it every day for breakfast

OAKFIELD That would be right up his alley wouldn't it But you know there's one thing bothers me

PATRICE What's that?

OAKFIELD Melody She acted very strangely after I'd had that drink I mean you saw her You don't suppose —

PATRICE Don't you start I've been all over that with Michael I think Melody must be some kind of weird nymphomaniac or something Did I tell you she kissed Jarvis?

OAKFIELD Good heavens! Jarvis?

PATRICE She seems to go around kissing everyone *(She looks around then leans towards him)* And in your case my love, I can understand just how easy that is to do

OAKFIELD Oh Snookums!

PATRICE Oh Pookie! *(They kiss PATRICE breaks away)* Now, here's what we've got to do Jarvis will never suspect you, so it's up to you to tell him you think the love potion works, and ask him to test it You've got to get him to agree to be the guinea-pig and drink some

OAKFIELD Then what?

PATRICE This time I'm going to convince him myself

OAKFIELD You? I'm not sure I like that idea

PATRICE Don't worry I have a feeling when it gets to the crunch he'll run a mile, and then, when I've finished, we'll get Tammy-Jo to make another pass at him and that should do it

OAKFIELD I hope you're right *(Voices off)* Shh! Here they are

(Enter MELODY and JARVIS from the west wing)

JARVIS It's turned into quite a nice evening madam There's even a little breeze blowing

PATRICE Is Mr Leadley in our room?

(JARVIS stops on his way down, MELODY continues on and exits to the kitchen)

JARVIS Yes, madam

PATRICE How's he making out?

JARVIS Perhaps an unfortunate choice of words madam He's lying down He seems to be feeling a little low

PATRICE Perhaps I'd better see if he's O K

(As she heads U S and exits to the west wing, she signals to OAKFIELD to talk to JARVIS)

OAKFIELD Oh yes Mr Jarvis, do you have moment?

JARVIS *(Stops by the kitchen door and turns)* Of course sir

OAKFIELD   Why don't you have a seat for a minute *(JARVIS just looks at him)* I mean, please sit down I'd like your opinion on something

JARVIS Really sir? *(Sits L chair)*

OAKFIELD Yes I've been thinking, and trying to put together a whole sequence of events this evening, and trying to figure out what it all means

JARVIS I'm afraid I don't quite follow you sir

OAKFIELD Bear with me It concerns the love potion Mr Leadley insists that after he drank some of it, Miss Melody - er - er - how can I put this delicately, let us say she became strongly attracted to him

JARVIS Yes, but —

OAKFIELD I know, you're going to say that anything Mr Leadley says or does in this regard is hardly to be relied on

JARVIS Exactly sir

OAKFIELD But in light of Miss Melody's subsequent attitude towards him, don't you think it's a little suspicious? Secondly, there is the rather remarkable behavior of Miss Tammy-Jo Harper with yourself after you had some of the potion

JARVIS Yes I did rather wonder about that

OAKFIELD Did you also wonder about Miss Melody kissing you immediately after the incident with Miss Harper? While the effects of the love potion might still have been present?

JARVIS I must admit, I hadn't thought too much about that

OAKFIELD Ah, but perhaps you should But let's proceed I prefer to ignore the claims of Mr Leadley that it was the love potion that made him assault Miss Winston, though a slight suspicion still lingers, but what is absolutely incontrovertible is that, after I was given some of the potion, both Mrs Leadley and Miss Melody — well, you saw Mrs Leadley yourself — I mean if you hadn't interrupted, she would have - er -

JARVIS Quite sir I must admit, I was somewhat surprised

OAKFIELD As well you should be Now, this is where the legal mind comes in Isolated events, which alone may mean very little, strung together, build a web of circumstantial evidence leading to one inevitable conclusion

JARVIS You mean? —

OAKFIELD Yes! I think the love potion works

JARVIS But it's impossible

OAKFIELD Oh no Improbable perhaps, but not impossible

JARVIS I can't believe it How can we be sure?

OAKFIELD I propose a test One that only you and I are aware of

JARVIS What sort of test?

OAKFIELD You drink it, and I observe

JARVIS Oh I'm not sure about that at all

OAKFIELD It would be simple enough and totally objective
We could have the whole thing settled in an hour or so

JARVIS If I agree, and I'm not saying I do, how would we do it?

OAKFIELD Simple In a little while, before everybody goes to
bed tonight, you drink some, and keep on drinking so it doesn't wear
off I'll try to observe the effects, from a discreet distance of course

JARVIS It sounds easy enough I suppose

OAKFIELD That's settled then *(Gets up and goes to the drinks
table, followed by JARVIS)* Now, let's put the potion in this empty
gin bottle so no one except the two of us will know what it is, and I'll
invite you to have a drink with us as soon as everyone gets back

*(Assisted by JARVIS, he pours the love potion out of the water jug
into the gin bottle, then refills the water jug from the thermos
PATRICE enters from the west wing and comes D.)*

JARVIS And how is Mr. Leadley madam?

PATRICE Oh, he'll survive He'll be down in a minute

JARVIS I see Well, *(He looks at OAKFIELD)* I'll be in the
kitchen if you need anything

(JARVIS exits to the kitchen)

PATRICE How did it go?

OAKFIELD Perfect He's going to do it, and you were right,
he's just about convinced

PATRICE O K All we need now is to get Tammy-Jo fired up
again and we're home free, — speak of the devil —

*(The front door opens and TAMMY-JO and MARY-LOU enter They
are wearing their rain gear which they take off)*

T-JO Hi everybody

PATRICE What's it like outside?

M-LOU Well, it's just about stopped raining, but the water level at the low bridge is still up around the four foot mark, and I don't think it'll fall much before morning Here, let me put these away

(She takes the raincoats, etc and exits to the kitchen TAMMY-JO heads up to B R 2)

PATRICE Miss Harper *(Follows her up and puts her arm round her shoulder)* You remember our little arrangement? Well here's what I'd like you to do —

(Still talking, they both exit to B R 2 and close the door Enter MELODY from the kitchen She is carrying a coffee pot She clutches it in both hands as though her life depended on it OAKFIELD, who is still standing just below the drinks table, comes L with outstretched arms)

OAKFIELD Let me get that
MELODY O K Thanks

(She simply lets go of the pot, and blissfully unaware of what might become of it, she immediately turns and returns to the kitchen OAKFIELD catches the pot just before it hits the floor He looks after her, shakes his head, then comes D L and puts the pot on the tray on the coffee table Enter JARVIS and MARY-LOU from the kitchen)

JARVIS I've made fresh coffee It's right here

M-LOU Thank you That sounds nice *(Comes D sits on the couch, R end, and pours herself a cup of coffee)* How about you Mr Oakfield?

OAKFIELD No thank you It's a little too close to bedtime for coffee for me, thank you

(Enter PATRICE from B R 2 She closes the door)

JARVIS *(Looking puzzled)* Ah, there you are madam I've just made some fresh coffee

PATRICE Thank you Jarvis Perhaps you'd care to join us?

(She comes D, sits on the couch L end and pours coffee OAKFIELD, who has remained D L by the front door, now crosses U R to the drinks table)

OAKFIELD I expect Jarvis might care for something a little stronger How about a gin and tonic Jarvis?

JARVIS Thank you sir, but I'm not really in the habit of — *(Sees OAKFIELD looking at him and holding up the gin bottle)* — oh yes, gin and tonic Thank you

PATRICE What about you Mr Oakfield?

OAKFIELD Not for me thank you, it's early to bed for me, just as soon as Mr Jarvis has his drink. *(He emphasizes the word drink and stares straight at PATRICE, who nods, confirming she's got the message)* I'll be off *(He has poured copious quantities of "gin" into a tall glass)* Here you are

(He hands the glass to JARVIS)

JARVIS Thank you *(He pauses and looks around the room)* Cheers! *(He drinks)*

OAKFIELD Well, goodnight everyone

(OAKFIELD exits to B R 1)

ALL Goodnight

M-LOU You know that sounds like a good idea I haven't slept in a real bed for ages *(Gets up and heads for the stairs)* It'll be really nice to

(As she passes JARVIS, who is standing just at the foot of the stairs, she stops dead in her tracks and leans close to him)

JARVIS Is something wrong miss?

(MARY-LOU leans over to him, breathing deeply, then without a word, suddenly turns away and runs into B R 2 slamming the door JARVIS looks at her and turns toward the kitchen)

PATRICE Goodness me, everyone left in a hurry Why don't you stay and finish your drink Jarvis?
JARVIS *(Turns from the kitchen door)* That's very kind of you madam, thank you

(He is about to sit in the L chair)

PATRICE Why don't you come over here on the couch I'm sure you'll be much more comfortable
JARVIS Thank you madam *(Sits on the couch, R end and sips his drink)* It has been rather a long day
PATRICE An interesting one too, wouldn't you say Jarvis?

(She inches towards him)

JARVIS Indeed madam
PATRICE I must admit I was surprised to find you and Tammy-Jo - er - you know
JARVIS Really madam, I thought that had taken place in the privacy of the study It seems that everyone in this house is aware of that unfortunate incident
PATRICE Well, we just happened to be by the door
JARVIS I see
(He looks quizzically at her and sips his drink)

PATRICE *(Now right next to him on the couch)* But it is rather strange isn't it?
JARVIS What is madam?

(PATRICE runs her finger around his neck as MARY-LOU, now in a

*bathrobe several sizes too large for her, comes out of B R 2,
pauses, leans over the railing towards the couch, sniffs the air,
then exits to the bathroom closing the door)*

PATRICE How everyone seems attracted to you today You're
surely not going to tell me it's all very normal for you?
JARVIS Are you implying madam that when you look at me the
phrase "magnificent pagan beast" does not spring readily to mind?
PATRICE Well, I never thought of you quite like that, but I
think perhaps there is something about you Jarvis
JARVIS About me madam?
PATRICE Yes, something irresistible
JARVIS Oh dear!
PATRICE Tell me Jarvis, do you have a particular girlfriend?
JARVIS Madam, all my girlfriends are particular

*(OAKFIELD enters from B R 1 and goes to the bathroom door He
tries the door, but it is locked Looking a little uncomfortable, he
smiles and nods at PATRICE and JARVIS, who are watching
him, then returns to B R 1 closing the door JARVIS, who has
been scrunched at the R end of the couch, seizes the moment to
escape by sliding over the R arm of the couch and standing up,
as MELODY enters from the kitchen)*

MELODY I've done all the dishes
JARVIS Thank you Melody

(He puts his glass on the small table)

MELODY Goodnight Mrs Leadley
PATRICE Goodnight Melody
MELODY *(Makes sure PATRICE is looking D S then gives
JARVIS a quick kiss on the lips)* Goodnight

*(She exits to the west wing PATRICE stands and continues her
pursuit of JARVIS as he backs away towards the center door)*

PATRICE This place is like Grand Central Station Let's go in the study where we can be alone Let me bring your drink for you

JARVIS I don't think I need any more of that drink madam, and being alone with you in the study is definitely not a good idea right now

PATRICE Oh Jarvis! Loosen up a bit What's the point of my feeling like this if you won't cooperate I've had it with you!

JARVIS If you say so madam, but I really don't recall the occasion

PATRICE Jarvis!

JARVIS I'm sorry madam I couldn't resist it

PATRICE Well, let's see if you can resist me

JARVIS Oh my dear Lord!

(As PATRICE reaches over the back of the small table for JARVIS' glass, he looks for a path of escape She turns U S towards him again and starts to advance in a sexy manner He opens the study door and rushes R into the powder room, slamming the door behind him PATRICE puts the glass down on the drinks table, crosses to the powder room door, and knocks)

PATRICE Jarvis

JARVIS *(Off)* What do you want?

PATRICE I want your hormones to come out and get some exercise

JARVIS *(Off)* Oh my dear Lord!

(OAKFIELD enters from B R 1 and tries the bathroom door It is still locked He looks around with his legs crossed, sees the open center door, comes down and goes into the study PATRICE hears someone coming and ducks behind the center door as OAKFIELD rushes to the powder room door It is locked OAKFIELD turns L , clearly in great discomfort, he sees PATRICE)

OAKFIELD Who's in there?

PATRICE Shh Jarvis What are you doing here? You're going to spoil everything

OAKFIELD I'm just looking for a bathroom

(MARY-LOU, still in her robe, comes out of the bathroom, and goes back into B R 2, leaving the door open OAKFIELD, now standing close to the center door, sees this and rushes past PATRICE He is halfway up the steps when TAMMY-JO, dressed as before, comes out of B R 2 She enters the bathroom, just half a step in front of him, and closes the door OAKFIELD, his legs crossed, his face showing extreme discomfort, gives a strangled moan, returns to B R 1 and closes the door MELODY enters from the west wing, comes D and exits to the kitchen PATRICE closes the center door then places herself immediately U S of the bed, against the R wall, and waits The powder room door slowly opens and JARVIS appears He does not see PATRICE and cautiously steps into the room PATRICE grabs him from behind and pulls him onto the bed with her, smothering him with kisses)

JARVIS Madam — madam!

PATRICE Now, you're mine, mine, mine!

(They remain entangled on the bed, PATRICE getting ever more passionate, JARVIS protesting feebly MICHAEL enters from the west wing, creeps furtively down the stairs and exits to the kitchen TAMMY-JO comes out of the bathroom and comes down to the center door OAKFIELD, who has heard the bathroom door open, opens the door of B R 1 and looks out He sees the open bathroom door, and half turns to close the door of B R 1 MARY-LOU enters from B R 2, goes in to the bathroom a half step ahead of him, and closes the door OAKFIELD gives a strangled cry, bends over, crosses his legs and shuffles off into B R 1, closing the door)

T-JO *(Opens the center door)* Well, excuse me!

(JARVIS manages, at last, to escape PATRICE's clutches and rushes up to TAMMY-JO.)

JARVIS. Miss Harper I've never been so pleased to see anyone in my life Things were beginning to get a little out of hand
PATRICE   *(Getting off the bed and straightening her clothes)* I swear, I don't know what came over me

(There is a loud thump, and a yell from the kitchen as MICHAEL staggers backwards through the door He is holding a broom between his legs He groans, holding his crotch as he falls to the floor PATRICE seizes the opportunity to escape and crosses L to watch him. JARVIS and TAMMY-JO follow her L into the living room)

JARVIS I see Miss Melody swept you off your feet sir!
PATRICE Come along Michael

(She pulls the broomstick from between his legs which produces another loud groan from MICHAEL and they exit to the west wing JARVIS picks up his drink and flops down in the L chair)

JARVIS You don't know just how glad I was to see you *(Drinks)*
T-JO Well, it's always nice to be appreciated, *(She leans over him from behind his chair)* and I'm sure you know just how much I appreciate you *(She runs her fingers through his hair)*
JARVIS You mean —? *(Puts his glass down)*
T-JO Yes She's paid me to do it again
JARVIS Shh They'll hear you Quickly, in the study *(They go into the study and close the door)* Now tell me
T-JO She wants me to put a move on you again
JARVIS Why a second time?
T-JO Beats me
JARVIS I don't know exactly what it is they're up to either, so we'd better go along with it, at least for a while, if you don't mind
T-JO What do you think we should do?

JARVIS Well, it's clear that they want us to believe the love potion works, so we'd better act as though it does

T-JO Why Mr Jarvis I do believe you're enjoying this

JARVIS I certainly did not enjoy being assaulted by Mrs Leadley, though in your case I'm reminded of the words of an old song which seem very appropriate

T-JO What's that?

JARVIS Something along the lines of "it's nice work if you can get it "

T-JO (Laughs) I bet she'll be checking up on us in a minute, so here we go Let's get the show on the road (She takes off her blouse, roughs up her hair a little, opens the center door slightly and calls out) Jarvis I must have you I cannot live without you, my love, my life

JARVIS (Sitting on the bed) Don't overdo it

(She sits next to him on the bed and breathes in deeply)

T-JO You know it's funny, but when I get close to you like this, it all seems to come very naturally

(OAKFIELD has entered from B R 1 He tries the bathroom door It is still locked He looks desperately around and comes down to the center door as TAMMY-JO signals to JARVIS that someone is coming, pushes him down on the bed and climbs all over him OAKFIELD taps lightly on the center door and pushes it open)

OAKFIELD Excuse me

T-JO (Sits up) Oh!

OAKFIELD I wondered if I could use the — (TAMMY-JO leaps off the bed, holds her blouse in front of her and dashes into the powder room, slamming the door behind her) — bathroom

JARVIS (Getting off the bed) You know, I do believe you're right, it really works, did you see her? Her hormones were working overtime You really saved me, your timing was perfect

(He puts his arm round Oakfield's shoulders and walks him into the *living room)*

OAKFIELD Timing be damned I needed to use the bathroom
JARVIS *(Ignoring the last remark)* Here, let's sit down for a
minute We need to talk about this

*(He steers OAKFIELD to the R chair, picks up his drink and sits in
the L chair)*

OAKFIELD I think perhaps sitting might be better, thank you

(He sits)

JARVIS *(Sipping his drink)* The possibilities are endless *(MARY-
LOU comes out of the bathroom, pauses, looks at JARVIS then exits to B
R 2, closing the door OAKFIELD sees the bathroom is now available
He stands and starts to move behind the chairs trying not to be impolite
and interrupt JARVIS, who never takes a breath)* Why, with the right
marketing set-up, we could have the whole world at our feet Mind you,
Mr Stancliffe was right, it could be dangerous If something like that
ever got into the wrong hands — (MELODY enters from the kitchen,
smiles at the two men, goes up the steps and into the bathroom as
OAKFIELD, in a last minute dash, is a half step behind her)* — well, you
can just imagine I think perhaps we'd have to dilute it I mean you saw
Miss Harper — *(He notices OAKFIELD at the top of the stairs, bent over
double and almost in tears)* I say, are you alright?

*(OAKFIELD just looks at him, gives a strangled cry and dashes into
B R 1 Enter TAMMY-JO from the powder room, now wearing
her blouse She crosses L into the living room, bends over the
back of the L chair and gives JARVIS a little peck on the cheek)*

T-JO How did I do?
JARVIS Sh Fine
T-JO *(Breathes in)* Mmm! You really do smell wonderful
JARVIS Cut that out

T-JO Alright dream boat
JARVIS I am not your dream boat

*(MELODY comes out of the bathroom, smiles at them and exits to the
west wing)*

T-JO I know, but I do love to tease you .

*(She turns, goes up the steps and enters the bathroom OAKFIELD,
who has heard the bathroom door open enters from B R 1 just
in time to see TAMMY-JO go in He stands for a second, looks
around, then, with a cry of anguish, he hobbles down the steps
with his legs crossed, runs D L and out of the front door Enter
PATRICE from the west wing)*

PATRICE You the only one still up Jarvis?
JARVIS *(Stands)* Indeed no madam In fact, I don't think
anyone is in bed yet
PATRICE Really? Not even Mr Oakfield?
JARVIS No madam, he appeared to be bursting to go outside I
believe he's taking a - er - er - a walk madam
PATRICE Really? *(She comes down closer to JARVIS who
backs hurriedly away)* It's turned into such a nice evening, I think
I'll join him
JARVIS I'm sure he'll be very relieved to see you madam

*(PATRICE exits front door, closing it JARVIS returns to his chair
Enter MELODY from the west wing)*
MELODY Hi I'm going to make some hot cocoa Like some?
JARVIS No thanks How's it going with Mr Leadley?
MELODY He's got more arms than an octopus

(She comes down behind JARVIS in the chair and breathes deeply)

JARVIS What are you doing?
MELODY Smelling you

JARVIS Don't you start

MELODY I don't care, you smell so good

JARVIS Melody I don't think — *(She comes down, sits on his lap, puts her arms round his neck and kisses him He eventually breaks contact)* Melody! *(He looks nervously around)* You shouldn't do that

MELODY I know, *(She gets up and touches the tip of his nose with her finger)* but you're so cute I can't help myself

(She exits to the kitchen)

JARVIS Cute! *(He picks up the "gin" and tonic, looks at it, then looks at the kitchen door, then the glass again)* NO! *(Then a long puzzled look at the kitchen door)*

(Enter MICHAEL from the west wing)

MICHAEL Oh, hi Jarvis Seen Melody?

JARVIS She's in the kitchen sir, *(MICHAEL heads for the kitchen)* and sir?

MICHAEL Yes?

JARVIS If I might be so bold as to offer you a little piece of advice sir?

MICHAEL Yes?

JARVIS I wonder if it ever occurred to you that there might just be the odd woman on this planet who, in fact, does not find you irresistible?

MICHAEL What are you getting at?

JARVIS Did it ever cross your mind that your advances to Miss Melody might be unwelcome?

MICHAEL What's your point?

JARVIS It's like talking to a gland! Never mind, but I warn you sir, she's a big girl and she knows how to take care of herself

(MICHAEL shrugs his shoulders and exits to the kitchen JARVIS gets up, goes into the study leaving the center door open and

*straightens out the bedclothes, then goes into the powder room
We hear MICHAEL yell in the kitchen He backs into the living
room, away from MELODY who advances on him with a huge
meat cleaver in her hand MICHAEL backs away with both
hands protecting his crotch)*

MICHAEL You wouldn't!
MELODY Try me

*(JARVIS, who has heard the yell, comes out of the powder room and
crosses to the center door, leaving it open)*

JARVIS Ah Mr Leadley Still holding on I see
MELODY If he comes near me again, he won't have anything
to hold on to!

(MICHAEL winces MELODY wheels about and exits to the kitchen)

JARVIS You can't say I didn't warn you sir
MICHAEL She'll come round, you'll see I'll find a way It
worked before and it'll work again You'll see

*(He exits to the west wing JARVIS returns to the L chair and sips
his "gin" and tonic as MARY-LOU, still dressed in the large
frumpish robe and bulky slippers, enters from B R 2 She holds
something behind her back She comes down, turns off the study
lights, closes the center door, comes behind JARVIS, leans over
him and inhales deeply)*

M-LOU Where is everyone?
JARVIS Mrs Leadley and Mr Oakfield are outside Tammy-
Jo's getting ready for bed I think, and who knows where the Melody
and Michael road show is on next
M-LOU We're alone then?
JARVIS For now at any rate
M-LOU Good

(T-JO comes out of the bathroom)

    T-JO Goodnight you guys

(She exits to B R 2)

    JARVIS Goodnight Miss
    M-LOU Goodnight Tammy-Jo I'll be in shortly

(She goes down to the front door and locks it)

    JARVIS What are you doing?
    M-LOU You'll see

(She turns off the living room lights There is a glow from the west wing and a subdued light from the reading lamp She strikes a pose, leaning against the front door She takes off and throws U S behind the couch, first one and then the other slipper She now produces from behind her back a pair of black four inch stiletto heel pumps First one black fishnet clad leg is revealed, and then the other as she puts on the shoes Next she removes her glasses, then pulls some pins out of her hair which cascades down over her shoulders She shakes her hair loose and slowly peels off the robe letting it slide off her shoulders and finally falling to the floor The totally transformed MARY-LOU is now revealed wearing the shoes, black fish-net tights and a low cut black lace teddy JARVIS sits, his eyes transfixed, his mouth open)

    M-LOU How do I look?
    JARVIS Like an evangelist's girl friend
    M-LOU Jarvis!
    JARVIS I'm sorry Miss Winston I just don't know what to say
    M-LOU Then don't say anything *(There is a knock at the front door)* Go away *(She comes R to JARVIS)* Ever since dinner, I've been going crazy thinking about you You know I've never felt this way before

(She leans close to him and takes a deep breath. Enter MICHAEL from the west wing He sees JARVIS and MARY-LOU, stops dead in his tracks, and watches from the corner of the west wing entrance on the landing JARVIS picks up his glass, holds it up and looks at it)

JARVIS It must be the love potion I still can't believe it, but it works

(MICHAEL reacts)

M-LOU *(Standing behind the chair and breathing deeply)* Oh Jarvis, all these years of waiting and wondering what it would be like Now I know
JARVIS *(Looking very uncomfortable.)* Now you know what?
M-LOU What it feels like to have a man I can call my own

(JARVIS gets up and moves away D R)

JARVIS I think perhaps you're moving a little too fast You don't have very much experience at this sort of thing do you?

(MARY-LOU follows him D R)

M-LOU None at all I've been saving myself

(JARVIS backs away U S L of the chairs)
JARVIS Well, perhaps you should save yourself a little while longer

(MARY-LOU follows him behind the chairs as MICHAEL ducks momentarily out of sight)

M-LOU But I don't want to save myself I want you! Now!
JARVIS *(Still moving)* Well now, that's probably not a good idea
M-LOU You don't know me very well, but if you did, you'd

know that I almost always have my way

JARVIS *(Still backing away, this time D S and L towards the front door)* Believe me it's just not a good idea for you to have your way with me

M-LOU *(Advancing relentlessly D S)* It's no good I want you I need you I'm going to have you You great big handsome hulk Now Tonight!

JARVIS Oh my dear Lord!

(He unlocks the front door and runs out)

M-LOU You can run, but you can't hide I mean it Tonight you belong to me!

(She exits and closes the front door)

MICHAEL *(Coming D)* I knew it It works! *(He goes to the kitchen door, listens for a moment then crosses R to the drinks table He picks up the water jug and looks at the kitchen door)* It worked before, and it'll work again *(Takes a drink directly from the water jug He wipes his lips with the back of his hand, primps a little as he crosses to the kitchen door which he opens a fraction)* Melody!

(He then lets go of the door, and hurriedly sits on the couch R side MELODY enters from the kitchen but remains in the doorway)

MELODY Yes?
(She switches on the L R lights)

MICHAEL Melody, I wondered if you could pour a drink for me please?

MELODY *(Suspicious)* I could, I suppose

MICHAEL Thank you I believe a small brandy would be nice

MELODY *(Still very dubious)* O K

(She goes to the drinks table)

MICHAEL You know Melody I've been thinking We seem to
have got off on the wrong foot today I think perhaps I need to
apologize to you I think I might have rushed things Do you think
we could, you know, start over?

MELODY *(Still doubtful)* O K Just don't come too near to me,
alright?

MICHAEL Oh dear, that's going to be a problem

MELODY What are you talking about?

MICHAEL Well you can't smell me if you're never near me

MELODY What?

MICHAEL I said I can't tell if you ever hear me

(MELODY comes D R of the couch with his drink)

MELODY Are you alright?

(MICHAEL leans deliberately towards her as he takes the glass)

MICHAEL Why don't you sit down and have a drink with me?

MELODY *(Backing away)* Look I said I was willing to start
over Let's just leave it at that Okay? Anyway, I've got some cocoa in
the kitchen

MICHAEL Why don't you bring it in here?

MELODY Are you sure you're on the level?

MICHAEL Absolutely, this is the new me

MELODY *(Still dubious)* Well, alright then

*(She exits to the kitchen MICHAEL runs up to the drinks table, takes
another long drink out of the water jug, then returns quickly to
the couch This time he sits on the L end and tries to look
nonchalant as MELODY enters with a plastic mug in her hand)*

MICHAEL Why don't you sit here? *(Indicates the R side of the
couch)*

MELODY O K then

(She sits MICHAEL slides R a little and leans over towards her as close as he can)

MICHAEL What a lovely evening it's turned into *(He breathes deeply)* Smell that air
MELODY Are you feeling sick or something?

(MICHAEL slides R further to get close to her)

MICHAEL I'm fine I just want to be near you I mean I want you to be near me

(MELODY gets up to avoid him)

MELODY Well I think that's near enough

(MICHAEL gets up and follows her as MELODY backs away towards the drinks table)

MICHAEL It's just not working Can you smell anything?
MELODY Yes Maybe a rat!
MICHAEL No, no Can't you smell something, maybe you left something on the stove

(He leans towards her MELODY leans forward a little and sniffs the air)

MELODY I don't think so

(She stops suddenly and looks at him with a puzzled expression on her face MICHAEL thinks the love potion is now working)

MICHAEL Melody, I'm convinced you and I could make beautiful music together

(He tries to grab her MELODY seizes the iron tongs off the railing and holds them towards him)

MELODY One more step and the only music you'll be hearing is the nutcracker suite!

(MICHAEL winces and holds his crotch)

MICHAEL You wouldn't
MELODY I'd enjoy it

(She advances on him)

MICHAEL Oh no!

(He runs out of the front door, leaving it open, followed by MELODY brandishing the tongs Enter TAMMY-JO from B R 2, now dressed in an attractive short silk robe She looks in the kitchen door)

T-JO Jarvis? *(She sees the open front door, comes D closes and locks it, then crosses U R to the center door She opens it, looks in, and turns on the light)* Jarvis?

(She starts to cross to the powder room and is halfway across when we hear VOICES OFF It is PATRICE and OAKFIELD As they start to climb in through the study window, TAMMY-JO hurls herself across the bed on to the floor D S , and crawls under the bed)

PATRICE I can't believe I'm climbing in windows in my own house in the middle of the night
OAKFIELD It's hardly the middle of the night dear
PATRICE You know what I mean
OAKFIELD I wonder who locked the front door?
PATRICE You were supposed to be watching Jarvis What in heaven's name were you doing outside?
OAKFIELD It was a very pressing situation

(They sit on the U S side of the bed)

PATRICE Did you see Tammy-Jo with Jarvis?
OAKFIELD Oh yes She was doing a great job, and he actually said to me that he believed the love potion was working
PATRICE That's it then Now, our next move — what's that?

(She goes to the window)

OAKFIELD What?
PATRICE Sh! There's somebody coming, we mustn't be caught together Quick, under the bed

(They both drop to the floor U S of the bed and get under it as TAMMY-JO comes out from under it on the D S side She avoids being seen by them by climbing quickly onto the bed as JARVIS appears in the window)

JARVIS Miss Harper, what on earth are you doing here?

(He climbs in through the window T-JO kneels up on the bed and signals to JARVIS that there is someone under it)

T-JO Waiting for you, oh lover of mine!
JARVIS What? — Oh, I see *(He mouths "WHO" and points under the bed)*
T-JO I know you don't want Mrs Leadley and Mr Oakfield. *(She emphasizes the names and points under the bed)* to know about us so why don't you close the door After all we have this big beautiful bed all to ourselves

(PATRICE and OAKFIELD stick their heads out D S of the bed, their eyes bulging and their mouths open)

JARVIS My dear Miss Harper, as an Englishman and a gentleman I'm afraid I could never take advantage of this situation You see, the only reason you find me attractive and irresistible is because of the love potion

T-JO *(Directing her voice for the benefit of PATRICE and OAKFIELD under the bed)* You mean it works?
JARVIS *(Following her lead)* I think it very possible

(PATRICE and OAKFIELD shake hands)

T-JO What makes you think so?

(JARVIS signals to her that they should go into the living room)

JARVIS Well, I had my suspicions earlier, but what totally convinced me was Mary-Lou

(They go into the living room, leaving the center door open, as PATRICE and OAKFIELD just look at each other with puzzled expressions They come out from under the bed and move to just below the center door to listen)

T-JO Mary-Lou?
JARVIS Mary-Lou
T-JO What about her?
JARVIS You're not going to believe this but after I drank some of the love potion, she smelled me and her hormones went into a feeding frenzy

(PATRICE and OAKFIELD react)

T-JO Mary-Lou?
JARVIS That's what I was doing coming in the window, trying to get away from her
T-JO Mary-Lou?
JARVIS Yes, for heaven's sake, Mary-Lou
T-JO That's incredible I mean we know Mary-Lou She's the sort of girl who would insist on a blind gynecologist You really mean—?
JARVIS Yes It would appear that the love potion works

(PATRICE and OAKFIELD react)

    T-JO Wow!
    JARVIS "Wow" is right "
    T-JO What are you going to do?
    JARVIS I have absolutely no idea
    T-JO Well, I'm going to bed *(Heads up, then turns)* Oh, I almost forgot I was looking for you to see if you could fix the window in our room It seems to be jammed somehow

(JARVIS follows her up)

    JARVIS You mean the one Melody —?
    T-JO I mean the one Melody opened
    JARVIS I see Alright let me see what I can do

(They both exit to B R 2 and close the door PATRICE and OAKFIELD sit at the foot of the bed)

    OAKFIELD What do you make of that?
    PATRICE I don't know
    OAKFIELD I mean, you didn't pay Mary-Lou to do anything did you?
    PATRICE Absolutely not
    OAKFIELD It doesn't make any sense *(Pause)* Could it really work?
    PATRICE You know, I've been thinking what Michael said about Melody
    OAKFIELD And don't forget Melody definitely came on to me, after I drank some
    PATRICE It would also explain Melody kissing Javis
    OAKFIELD Could we have been so wrong?
    PATRICE Well if we are, and it really works, we certainly don't want Jarvis to end up with it It's got to be worth ten times what this ranch is worth Quick, there's somebody coming

(They hide on the floor D S of the bed as MARY-LOU enters through the window)

M-LOU Come on out Jarvis I saw you, I know you're in here *(She looks in the powder room then crosses L into the living room and opens the kitchen door She calls in)* Jarvis?
OAKFIELD *(As they get up and return to just below the center door to listen)* Did you see what she was wearing?
PATRICE Sh!

(JARVIS enters from B R 2 and closes the door)

M-LOU Jarvis!
JARVIS *(Coming down)* Are you feeling alright now Miss Winston?

(He picks up MARY-LOU's robe and holds it out for her)

M-LOU *(Ignoring the robe)* I was feeling alright before
JARVIS Yes, but you were, well, you know
M-LOU *(Now close to him and breathing deeply)* Yes, I know, and I still am
JARVIS Oh dear! *(MARY-LOU flings her arms round JARVIS and tries to kiss him as they fall over the R arm of the couch PATRICE and OAKFIELD watch through the center door as JARVIS eventually breaks away)* Miss Winston, you really cannot go around doing this sort of thing
M-LOU I can't seem to help myself
JARVIS *(Backing away, up the stairs)* I think you really should ask yourself why you never felt this way about me before
M-LOU I must have been blind You're everything any woman could want, and anyway I don't intend to ask I intend to take

(She follows him up)

JARVIS Oh my dear Lord! *(He has backed his way up the stairs*

*and inched L He now has his back to the door of B R 2 He knocks
on the door)* Miss Harper?

M-LOU You don't need her I intend to have you all to myself

T-JO *(Opens the door of B R 2)* Yes?

JARVIS I need a little assistance here

T-JO You mean she's - er - still - ?

JARVIS Yes, she's shifted into overdrive again

T-JO Mary-Lou, I think maybe I should try to explain to you
how this boy-girl thing works, and anyway, it's late Let's get you to
bed before you get into trouble

M-LOU I think I like being in trouble

T-JO *(To JARVIS)* I see what you mean *(She takes Mary-Lou's
robe from JARVIS)* Come along Mary-Lou

(She takes MARY-LOU by the arm and steers her into B R 2)

JARVIS Thank you

T-JO You're welcome Goodnight

JARVIS Goodnight

*(TAMMY-JO and MARY-LOU exit to B R 2, closing the door
JARVIS comes down, goes to the drinks table, pours himself a
soft drink then slumps down in the L chair with a big sigh
PATRICE and OAKFIELD, hearing someone outside the
window, dash down and hide D S of the bed again, as MELODY
enters through the window She is still carrying the tongs She
enters the living room leaving the center door open PATRICE
and OAKFIELD come back up to the center door to listen)*

MELODY Oh, hi Jarvis How's it going?

(She puts the tongs back on the railing)

JARVIS It is going, as you put it, quite well, I suppose Where's
the octopus?

MELODY *(Laughs)* Oh you mean Mr Leadley Heaven knows

(She stands behind his chair and begins to massage his neck and shoulders) You look exhausted

JARVIS Well, I've just had quite an experience with Mary-Lou

MELODY *(Breathes deeply)* You know you really do smell awfully good *(She bends over and kisses him PATRICE and OAKFIELD react)* What sort of experience with Mary-Lou?

JARVIS Well, I don't think she really knows how to go about this love potion thing, and she's just gone overboard I mean she's gone quite berserk

MELODY I'm sure you managed alright *(She breathes deeply again and closes her eyes)* You know I can't live without you don't you

(PATRICE and OAKFIELD react)

JARVIS Melody my dear, another time perhaps *(He stands)* Come on I'll see you safely to your room

(They exit to the west wing PATRICE and OAKFIELD come L into the living room and sit on the couch)

OAKFIELD Did you see what Mary-Lou was wearing?

PATRICE You've already said that What she was wearing was only part of it She's totally transformed I've never seen anything like it

OAKFIELD Did you see Melody again? She could hardly keep her hands off him

PATRICE How much of that stuff did he drink?

OAKFIELD I don't know, but we agreed he should keep drinking it, so the effects wouldn't wear off

PATRICE I can't get over Mary-Lou

OAKFIELD You know, all this is leading to one inescapable conclusion

PATRICE Yes?

OAKFIELD There appears to be something in that concoction *(He indicates the drinks table)* that really does affect people

PATRICE But that's incredible

OAKFIELD Nevertheless, incredible or not, it appears to me

that the love potion actually works
      PATRICE Absolutely amazing

(Pause)

      OAKFIELD Now what?
      PATRICE We've got to get our hands on Jarvis' 50%
      OAKFIELD That's going to be easier said than done We've
clearly done too good a job He's convinced it works

*(There is a pounding at the front door MICHAEL's voice is heard
      PATRICE goes down, unlocks and opens it MICHAEL enters)*

      MICHAEL Boy, am I pleased to see you
      PATRICE That makes a change, anyway what were you doing
outside at this time of night?
      MICHAEL Trying to get away from Melody

*(PATRICE sits back on the couch as Michael goes up to the drinks
      table)*

      PATRICE You? Trying to get away from Melody?
      MICHAEL Well, you see, I thought I would try the love potion
again to see if it really worked
      PATRICE And?
      MICHAEL *(Fixing himself a drink)* It didn't work at all and
Melody got kinda mad
      PATRICE It didn't work? Now I'm really confused
      OAKFIELD Wait a minute, what did you drink it out of?
      MICHAEL This of course

(He holds up the water jug)

      OAKFIELD That was water, the love potion is in the gin bottle
      MICHAEL What? No wonder Melody got mad
      PATRICE Michael, come and sit down for a minute *(He comes*

D to sit on the L   chair) While you were out gallivanting with Melody, Mr Oakfield and I have pretty much established that the love potion, in fact, does work

MICHAEL Hot dog! I knew it I told you and you didn't believe me

OAKFIELD The problem is, Jarvis owns 50% of Amelixco

MICHAEL Yes, but we own the other half

PATRICE We've got to find a way to get him to part with his half

MICHAEL How do you propose to do that?

PATRICE Well, there might be a way

MICHAEL How?

PATRICE You have to learn to think like a woman

MICHAEL Don't try to make me think like a woman

PATRICE You couldn't anyway, your brains are in the wrong part of your anatomy Mr Oakfield, can you draw up a contract for Jarvis to sign over his 50% of Amelixco in exchange for this ranch?

OAKFIELD Yes, but I don't have a typewriter or anything

PATRICE If you just wrote it out, would it be legal?

OAKFIELD Of course

PATRICE Alright Do it

OAKFIELD Are you sure? I mean this ranch is worth a very large sum of money

PATRICE Of course I'm sure Once we've got control of the love potion, we can buy ten ranches

(OAKFIELD gets up)

OAKFIELD Well, if you're absolutely certain I'll get to work It won't take long, just a simple sales agreement should do it Now you're quite certain this is what you want?

PATRICE I'm positive

(OAKFIELD exits B R 1)

MICHAEL This is fantastic The whole world will beat a path to our door We'll be rich beyond our wildest dreams

PATRICE. First we have to persuade Jarvis to cooperate

MICHAEL Oh yes How in heaven's name are we going to do that?

PATRICE It won't be easy We've done too good a job He's convinced it works too

MICHAEL Can't we unconvince him

PATRICE I doubt it now I think our best bet is to persuade him it's too dangerous, too volatile, too explosive Make him feel he'd just be better off with the ranch

MICHAEL I'd never go for that

PATRICE No, I don't suppose you would But you're not him and he's not you Anyway it's worth a try, so let's get him in here right away

MICHAEL What now? Tonight?

PATRICE Yes I think so We need to strike while the iron is hot In this case while Mary-Lou is still hot Jarvis was definitely looking very frazzled a few minutes ago

MICHAEL Alright, where is he?

PATRICE He took Melody to her room

MICHAEL *(Stands)* I'll go and get him

PATRICE *(Stands)* I think not Michael I'll go

(She exits to the west wing MICHAEL watches her go, then goes to the drinks table, picks up the gin bottle and is about to pour a drink from it)

PATRICE *(Off)* And stay away from that gin bottle!

(MICHAEL hurriedly puts it down, pauses for a moment, looks towards the west wing, then takes a swig right out of the bottle He primps a little, takes a comb out of his pocket then goes up and exits to the bathroom Enter PATRICE and JARVIS from the west wing)

JARVIS You're absolutely right madam, it really has been a most extraordinary day

PATRICE Come and sit down Jarvis I want to talk to you about the love potion

JARVIS Really madam It is quite amazing isn't it

(He sits L chair)

PATRICE How do you feel about it Jarvis?

(She sits couch R side)

JARVIS I'm not sure I'm still reeling both from the effects and the implications of it all

PATRICE You know, life is never going to be the same again

JARVIS I'm not sure I follow you madam

PATRICE Well, we're all going to have to live with fame and publicity now I don't think any of us will be able to enjoy much privacy again in our lives

JARVIS I hadn't really thought of that Oh dear!

PATRICE What's the matter?

JARVIS Well, I think I'm a little too old for fame and publicity All I ever really wanted was to live out my days here in peace and quiet

(MICHAEL, unseen by either JARVIS or PATRICE, comes out of the bathroom, primps a little and exits to the west wing)

PATRICE Funny you should say that because Mr Leadley and I were just talking about the same thing We feel almost the opposite The solitude of this ranching life-style is not really what we were cut out for

JARVIS But it's a wonderful life out here madam

PATRICE For you yes For us no You've seen Michael, he wants the city, the bright lights He wants the love potion

JARVIS Well I'm not sure I do

PATRICE What?

JARVIS If tonight is any indication of what it can do to people's lives, I don't think I want any part of it

PATRICE Why Jarvis —

JARVIS Don't misunderstand me madam, I definitely do want the money that the love potion will undoubtedly bring, it's just that I'm not looking forward to what we'll have to do to get it

(MICHAEL backs on to the stage from the west wing, followed by MELODY She has a huge pair of cattle castrating shears in her hands MICHAEL's hands are protecting his crotch)

JARVIS Ah Mr Leadley, still holding a grievance I see

MELODY Is that what it's called?

MICHAEL I just wanted to be near you, that's all

MELODY *(Advancing)* Come on then, come near to me

MICHAEL I don't think so *(To PATRICE, as he backs down the stairs)* I don't think it's working

MELODY Just let me get near you and it'll never work again

MICHAEL *(Backs away D L towards the front door)* Are you just going to sit there?

PATRICE No, I think I'm going to applaud

MICHAEL Look at her, she means it Something's wrong I really drank some this time, out of the gin bottle

(At this point, MELODY has come very close to MICHAEL She stops dead in her tracks, gazes into his eyes and breathes in deeply She drops the shears MICHAEL backs away just a little, a look of disbelief on his face MELODY, still breathing deeply, advances This time the mood has changed She kisses him lightly on the cheek then turns and goes up the stairs They all watch as she heads L to the west wing She stops, strikes a slinky sexy pose, beckons to MICHAEL and exits MICHAEL salivating starts to follow)

PATRICE Just where do you think you're going?

MICHAEL *(Stops dead in his tracks)* Nowhere?

PATRICE That's right

(MICHAEL sits on the couch, L end)

JARVIS Oh dear! Is this an example of what life is going to be like?
PATRICE I'm afraid so, but perhaps there is a very simple solution
JARVIS Madam?
PATRICE What would you say to signing over your 50% of Amelixco, in exchange for this ranch?
JARVIS You mean I'd own the ranch?
PATRICE Yes
JARVIS I don't know madam I'd have to give it some thought
PATRICE Don't you see Jarvis We could own the love potion, go back to the city, start the manufacturing and marketing process, and you could stay right here You'd be the owner of this ranch, your lifestyle not interrupted or changed at all You said yourself, that's what you wanted
JARVIS Well, when you put it like that it certainly sounds very tempting
PATRICE What do you think Jarvis?
JARVIS I'm not sure madam This is a very serious decision

(Enter MARY-LOU from B R 2 She now has her robe back on She creeps out, so as not to disturb TAMMY-JO, silently closes the door, turns and sees everyone looking at her)

M-LOU Mr Leadley Mrs Leadley I thought you'd all gone to bed
PATRICE No, we were just having a little chat with Jarvis
M-LOU Oh I see

(She just stands there)

PATRICE *(Eventually)* Is there something we can do for you?
M-LOU Not really I was hoping to see Jarvis
JARVIS Well?

M-LOU I mean - alone
JARVIS Oh dear!
PATRICE That's alright Mr Leadley and I were just going to bed anyway *(Gets up)* Weren't we Michael?
MICHAEL What?
PATRICE Miss Winston wants to be alone with Mr Jarvis
JARVIS Oh dear!
MICHAEL Oh I see *(Gets up)* Yes, of course Goodnight
JARVIS You don't have to go you know
PATRICE Goodnight everyone

(PATRICE and MICHAEL exit to the west wing MARY-LOU watches them go then comes slowly down the stairs)

JARVIS Where's Tammy-Jo?
M-LOU Asleep I hope
JARVIS Did she talk to you?
M-LOU What about?
JARVIS You know, this boy-girl thing
M-LOU Oh that Yes Isn't it wonderful
JARVIS Isn't what wonderful?
M-LOU This boy-girl thing

(She has now come down below the chair, and with her back to the audience opens her robe)

JARVIS Mary-Lou, please, you don't understand There's no need to do this I'm afraid you still haven't got the right idea This is not how it works
M-LOU *(Wriggling and twisting beneath the robe)* I know exactly how it works
JARVIS What are you doing? *(Still with her back to the audience, MARY-LOU finally produces the black lace teddy, twirls it above her head and throws it away)* Oh my dear Lord!

(OAKFIELD enters from B R 1 with legal papers in his hand He

sees MARY-LOU Stands open mouthed for a second)

OAKFIELD Oh my —

(He retreats hastily back into B R 1 closing the door MARY-LOU hurls herself at JARVIS, and, with her back to the audience, holds her robe open and smothers him with kisses JARVIS eventually escapes from MARY-LOU's clutches, picks up the teddy and hands it to her)

JARVIS I think you ought to put this on
M-LOU Why Jarvis! *(Advances on him)* I'll put this on for you anytime
JARVIS That's not what I meant
M-LOU *(Sexily)* Oh I know what you meant
JARVIS Not that I want you to put some real clothes on
M-LOU I don't think I'm ever going to wear real clothes again

(JARVIS continues to back away from her, D S L toward the front door)

JARVIS Mary-Lou This is all wrong
M-LOU I think I like wrong
JARVIS Oh my dear Lord! What have we done? *(MARY-LOU continues to advance with the teddy draped seductively over one shoulder)* Miss Harper! Help!*

(He runs out of the front door, followed by MARY-LOU just as TAMMY-JO comes out of B R 2)

T-JO Mary-Lou wait

(She hurries after them, out of the front door and closes it behind her Enter MELODY and MICHAEL from the west wing They have their arms round each other as MELODY gazes adoringly at him)
MELODY Let's find a place where we can be alone together

MICHAEL It works, it really works

MELODY What do you mean, Michael?

MICHAEL Oh, nothing my dear Why don't we go into the study, no one will disturb us there

MELODY Oh Michael!

(MICHAEL opens the center door for MELODY to enter, turns quickly back to the drinks table, has a quick swig out of the gin bottle, then follows her into the study, carefully looks behind him to be sure they haven't been seen, and closes the door)

MICHAEL Alone at last, let the games begin!

(He advances R towards her, his groping hands outstretched MELODY fends him off gently)

MELODY Tell you what, why don't you get ready, while I go and slip into something a little more comfortable?

MICHAEL You mean — ?

MELODY Yes, I'm going to change and do my hair

MICHAEL You don't have to I like it that way

MELODY I get the distinct impression you like it every way I'll be back in five minutes

(She avoids his clutches again, opens the center door, turns, blows him a kiss, closes the door and exits to the west wing MICHAEL, salivating and singing to himself, turns down the bed, fluffs the pillows, closes the drapes, opens the center door, looks around, takes another swig out of the gin bottle, returns to the study, closes the center door and exits jauntily into the powder room closing the door Enter PATRICE from the west wing She comes R and knocks on the door of B R 1 OAKFIELD opens the door PATRICE takes a quick look around as OAKFIELD takes one step D S)

PATRICE Oh Pookie!

OAKFIELD Oh Snookums!

(They embrace)

PATRICE Have you got the papers ready?
OAKFIELD Yes, it's all done Is Jarvis ready to sign?
PATRICE I'm not sure, but I think he's close
OAKFIELD Where is he?
PATRICE I don't know, we left him alone with Mary-Lou, in the hopes she would push him over the top, but everything seems quiet I think maybe everyone's gone to bed and we'll have to try again in the morning
OAKFIELD Where's your husband?
PATRICE I've no idea, and I'm past caring He's probably off gallivanting somewhere with Melody
OAKFIELD So you're alone?
PATRICE Oh Pookie!
OAKFIELD Oh Snookums!

(They embrace)

PATRICE Why don't I, you know, come in?
OAKFIELD Oh Snookums there's just one tiny little bed
PATRICE Oh *(Pause)* I know, the study Why don't I slip into something a little more comfortable and I'll meet you there in five minutes
OAKFIELD Oh Snookums!
PATRICE Oh Pookie!

(They embrace, then break apart They blow kisses to each other as PATRICE exits to the west wing, and OAKFIELD returns to B R 1 closing the door Enter JARVIS through the study window He is in a hurry, looking behind him and dives under the bed, just in time to avoid being seen by MARY-LOU, who follows him in the window She is dressed as before in the robe and carrying the teddy Enter MICHAEL from the powder room)

M-LOU Oh hello

(She puts the teddy behind her back)

MICHAEL Hello *(Pause)* What are you doing here?
M-LOU I'm looking for Jarvis
MICHAEL I see Excuse me

*(He crosses L in front of her, cautiously opens the center door and looks out
He steps into the living room and takes a swig from the gin bottle [SEE
AUTHOR'S NOTE] He returns to the study and doesn't have time to
close the door before MARY-LOU is all over him)*

MICHAEL It's unbelievable
M-LOU I know
MICHAEL *(Fending her off and looking nervously out of the
study door)* Do you think I might take a rain check?
M-LOU What?

*(Enter MELODY from the west wing, looking very attractive in a
short silk robe MICHAEL sees her headed for the kitchen and
quickly closes the study door as MELODY exits to the kitchen)*

MICHAEL I never thought I'd live to hear myself say this, but
this is too much You've got to go
M-LOU *(Close to him and breathing deeply)* But I don't want to go

(She tries to kiss him, as he gently pushes her out of the window)

MICHAEL Later, later I promise I'll see you later

*(MARY-LOU exits window In a frantic hurry, MICHAEL takes off
his shoes, socks, shirt and pants, hurls them into the powder
room, closes the door, leaps into bed, moves to the D S side,
turns off the bedside light, and pulls the covers right up over his
head MARY-LOU creeps furtively back in the study window,*

doesn't notice the figure under the covers, tip-toes to the study door, opens it slightly and peeks out She sees OAKFIELD, now wearing his robe, who has entered from B R 1, come down the steps and is about to turn R toward the study She silently closes the door and dives under the bed as OAKFIELD enters the study He sees the figure in the bed and comes U S of the bed He takes off his robe revealing his underwear He is wearing a white undershirt and white boxer shorts with large red hearts all over them He playfully tickles the figure under the covers which wriggles After a whole series of wriggles and giggles, he finally gets into bed U S side There is a frantic movement under the covers JARVIS and MARY-LOU put their heads out from under the bed, D S side, eyes bulging toward the audience MARY-LOU then grabs JARVIS, and kissing him frantically, they disappear again under the bed OAKFIELD and MICHAEL throw off the covers as they sit up in bed and yell MICHAEL is kneeling with his hands on OAKFIELD OAKFIELD hits him in the crotch with his elbow OAKFIELD screams and dives head first out of the window as MICHAEL falls on the floor on the D S side of the bed groaning in agony Eventually he gets up, and limps painfully to the kitchen door JARVIS tries to escape on the D S side of the bed, but is pulled back under by MARY-LOU)

MICHAEL *(Opens the kitchen door a fraction and calls in)* Melody

(MELODY appears in the doorway and gives him a peck on the cheek)

MELODY I'm nearly ready, go and get into bed lover-boy

(She disappears back into the kitchen)

MICHAEL *(To himself as he crosses R)* Lover-boy! Did you hear that? This is it!

(He stops by the drinks table, takes yet another swig out of the gin

*bottle, goes into the study, gets into bed, moves to the D S side
and pulls the covers right up   Enter PATRICE from the west
wing   She is wearing silk pajamas and an open peignoir type
robe   She comes D   crosses R   enters the study and closes the
door   She sees the figure in the bed, slips off her robe and gets
into bed U S   side   There is a frantic giggling and wriggling,
then a sudden stillness under the covers, as PATRICE and
MICHAEL sit bolt upright in bed)*

MICHAEL You!
PATRICE You!
MICHAEL What are you doing here?
PATRICE I was going to ask you the same thing
MICHAEL I asked first
PATRICE Well, - er - er - I came down to see what had
happened to Jarvis and Mary-Lou

(JARVIS and MARY-LOU put their heads out and look at each other)

MICHAEL And?
PATRICE And what?
MICHAEL And why did you get into bed?
PATRICE Ah that, yes, well, - er - er – I knew it was you and
thought I'd surprise you
MICHAEL Well you did that alright
PATRICE And you?
MICHAEL Me?
PATRICE Yes, you
MICHAEL What?
PATRICE What are you doing here?
MICHAEL Well, - er - everyone seemed to be moving around
the house making noises, so I thought the study would be peaceful
and quiet and I could get some sleep
PATRICE I see *(Pause)* Why don't we get back to our room?

(MARY-LOU hauls JARVIS back under the bed)

MICHAEL Good idea

(They both get out of bed PATRICE puts on her robe They both head up to the west wing)

PATRICE You know I really wanted to try to get to Jarvis tonight, before the love potion wears off

MICHAEL The sooner the better I guess I just can't wait till it's all ours

PATRICE I'll just bet you can't

MICHAEL And what's that supposed to mean?

PATRICE Michael, it's me you're talking to Do you think I don't know you've been running around all these years?

MICHAEL I resent that I don't deny it, I just resent it

(They both exit talking to the west wing)

JARVIS *(Trying to escape, D S side of the bed)* Mary-Lou stop We can't stay here all night

M-LOU Why not?

JARVIS Why not!

M-LOU That's right, I've never had so much fun in my life Tell you what, turn off the light and turn me on

(She grabs him again)

JARVIS Mary-Lou let me try to explain once again

(She pulls him under the bed MELODY has entered from the kitchen She is dressed as before, but now carries a length of coiled rope, and a pair of jumper cables She enters the study as JARVIS and MARY-LOU duck under the bed, goes into the powder room and closes the door Enter TAMMY-JO and OAKFIELD from the front door OAKFIELD is in a pitiful state He has mud on his face, bits of shrubbery hanging from him, his undershirt is torn, his glasses awry)

T-JO Come along Mr Oakfield What in heaven's name were
you doing out there?

OAKFIELD It's not supposed to work that way

T-JO What?

OAKFIELD The love potion, it's not supposed to work on men

T-JO What?

OAKFIELD Well it's supposed to work on men, but I mean it's
not supposed to work on men, on men

T-JO I have no idea what you're talking about I think maybe
you should get back to your room

OAKFIELD That's a good idea I think I'll just get cleaned up a
little

*(He exits to B R 1, while TAMMY-JO picks up the tray, coffee cups,
etc and exits to the kitchen Enter MICHAEL from the west
wing, still in his underwear He comes D , looks in the study,
sees no one, crosses L to the kitchen door and listens He grins,
rushes back to the drinks table, takes a swig out of the gin bottle
and hurries back to the kitchen door He primps a little then
goes in There is a pause, followed by a loud thump and a yell
from MICHAEL TAMMY-JO enters grinning from ear to ear
and exits to B R 2 Michael enters doubled over and holding his
crotch Enter MELODY from the powder room, leaving the door
open She has the length of rope in her hand, it has a large
noose at one end She opens the study door, and, keeping the
rope behind her back, beckons sexily to MICHAEL He limps
right and she opens the study door for him As he enters, his
hands still holding his crotch, she closes the door then slips the
noose over his shoulders, pulls it tight, trapping his arms at his
sides, then, quick as a flash, pushes him down on the bed He
falls on his back, legs together, knees bent, but in the air She
quickly takes a few turns on the rope around his knees and lower
legs, then a couple of turns around his wrists which are together
pinioned in front of his body)*

MICHAEL What are you doing?

MELODY What do you think I'm doing? I'm going to fix you once and for all

MICHAEL What do you mean fix me?

MELODY You may think I'm dumb I may never have been to college, and I'm certainly no veterinarian, but I've lived on this ranch long enough to know what fix means

(She goes into the powder room as JARVIS and MARY-LOU look out from under the D S side of the bed They look questioningly at each other MELODY reappears immediately with the jumper cables and comes down below the bed as JARVIS and MARY-LOU duck under it MICHAEL, on his back, watches in horror as MELODY unscrews the light bulb from the bedside lamp)

MICHAEL I think it must have worn off *(MELODY clamps one end of the jumper cables into the light socket)* Oh no! *(MELODY takes the other end of the jumper cables and is now standing poised over MICHAEL, one clamp in each hand)* Please! What are you going to do?

MELODY If you haven't guessed by now, you're in for quite a shock!

(MICHAEL screams PATRICE, dressed as before, has entered from the west wing and crept down, somewhat furtively, to the study door She stops outside the door and primps a little She hears the scream and opens the door)

PATRICE Melody! Michael! What's going on here?

(There is a stunned silence)

JARVIS *(From under the bed)* Help!
PATRICE *(Looks under the bed)* Jarvis?

(JARVIS comes out from under the bed His hair is messed up, his tie awry, his vest unbuttoned, his shirt tail out)

JARVIS That's it I can't take any more of this *(MARY-LOU*

follows him out from under the bed) I'm ready to sign Mrs Leadley,
you take the love potion, I'll take the ranch
    PATRICE Right, I'll just get Mr Oakfield

(She heads up to B R 2 MARY-LOU follows her out of the study,
    ruffles JARVIS' hair as she passes and sits on the couch L end
    PATRICE knocks on the door of B R 1 and OAKFIELD appears)

    PATRICE Would you bring the papers please Mr Jarvis would
like to sign them now

(OAKFIELD disappears from sight MELODY looks at JARVIS, grins
    and positions the jumper cables again Michael screams)

    JARVIS *(Who has been straightening his clothing)* Melody
Let's not jump to conclusions Please don't start anything *(She stops)*
I think perhaps you should untie him It's all over

(She starts to untie him JARVIS enters the living room and sits in
    the L chair OAKFIELD, Now wearing shirt and pants,
    reappears with legal papers and a pen)

    OAKFIELD We'll need two witnesses *(Knocks on the door of*
B R 2 TAMMY-JO appears)* Perhaps you'd be kind enough to
witness some signatures miss
    T-JO Of course

(PATRICE, TAMMY-JO AND OAKFIELD come down PATRICE sits
    in the R chair, TAMMY-JO sits on the couch R end From
    behind the chairs, OAKFIELD hands papers and pen first to
    JARVIS and then to PATRICE)

    OAKFIELD Mr Jarvis, would you sign here, and here, and
once more here Thank you Now, Mrs Leadley, here, and here and
here Thank you Now we'll need the witnesses

(He moves L behind the couch MELODY, having untied MICHAEL, comes into the living room, ruffles JARVIS' hair as she passes and exits to the west wing MICHAEL, now free, follows her, takes a swig out of the gin bottle, pauses, then pours the rest over his head, and exits to the west wing Everyone watches)

JARVIS You'd think he'd learn wouldn't you
OAKFIELD *(Handing the papers over the back of the couch)* Miss Harper, perhaps you would oblige, here, here, and here, and Miss Winston *(They sign)* There That does it *(He crosses R to the chairs)* One copy for you Mrs Leadley, and one for you Mr Jarvis I think I should congratulate both parties
JARVIS That's all we need to do?
OAKFIELD Absolutely These are totally binding legal agreements Of course we have to transfer title of the ranch to you Mr Jarvis, and register the stock in Amelixco to you Mrs Leadley, but these are mere formalities Both sales agreements are now completed
PATRICE It's done then?
OAKFIELD It's done

(There is a tremendous thump from the west wing, followed by a yell from MICHAEL Everybody turns and looks at the west wing entrance MELODY enters, carrying a baseball bat on her shoulder, smiles at everyone and exits to the kitchen)

PATRICE Come along, Mr Oakfield, you and I are finally going to have that little chat with my husband We'll be leaving first thing in the morning Jarvis

(They head U S towards the west wing)

OAKFIELD Don't forget, you all need to come into my office
PATRICE Goodnight ladies *(She pauses and bows slightly to JARVIS)* Jarvis
JARVIS *(Stands)* Madam
OAKFIELD Goodnight

.

M-LOU Goodnight
T-JO Goodnight

*(PATRICE and OAKFIELD exit to the west wing JARVIS follows
them to the foot of the stairs, TAMMY-JO gets up and moves to
his R MARY-LOU gets up and moves to his L They stand there
for a moment with their backs to the audience Finally they turn
D S)*

JARVIS It's done I've got the ranch
T-JO Oh Jarvis, that's wonderful
JARVIS That just leaves a couple of odds and ends to tidy up
(He produces a check from his vest pocket) Here you are my dear
(He hands it to TAMMY-JO) A check for $25,000 as we agreed
T-JO You don't have to pay me I would have helped you for
free
JARVIS No A deal is a deal You know I couldn't have done it
without you
T-JO Thank you Jarvis, and Mrs Leadley thought she could buy
me for $5,000 What a nerve
JARVIS *(Turns to MARY-LOU)* And you too my dear Here's
your check for $25,000 You really were terrific
M-LOU You don't think I overdid it do you?
JARVIS *(Laughs)* Well the thought did cross my mind at the
time, but all's well that ends well We pulled it off
M-LOU Incidentally what was the love potion?
JARVIS Just water
M-LOU But whatever gave you the idea?
JARVIS Well, I knew Amelixco was a real company, and even
though it hadn't any value, I knew how Mr Stancliffe had
bequeathed the shares and that's how it started Strangely enough
though, although I suppose I can take credit for the planning of
today's events, the original idea about a love potion wasn't mine
T-JO Well, whoever thought of it was brilliant I mean it was a
stroke of genius

(There is a huge crash in the kitchen and MELODY enters)

MELODY Oops!

(JARVIS holds out his hands, MELODY crosses R and he takes her hands in his)

MELODY I think that's about the last of the dishes

JARVIS Never mind *(He turns to MARY-LOU and TAMMY-JO)* Let me introduce you to the genius whose brilliant mind conceived the love potion

M-LOU Melody?

T-JO Melody?

JARVIS Melody!

MELODY Well, I just thought of it, Jarvis organized it all

JARVIS Now Melody, don't be so modest, you had to do your part with Oakfield and Michael

MELODY I was just lucky to overhear Mrs Leadley say they were going to give some love potion to Mr Oakfield

M-LOU And Michael?

MELODY It didn't take a nobel prize winner to figure out he'd be drinking it all day anyway

JARVIS You were fantastic

MELODY Oh Jarvis!

JARVIS Melody, do you remember how I promised to take care of you?

MELODY Yes

JARVIS Well, I will Forever But you do know the first thing we're going to do after we're married?

MELODY What?

JARVIS Hire a maid

(They embrace and —)

CURTAIN

AUTHOR'S NOTES

Page 44   While Melody's subsequent behavior is determined by the fact that, as she enters, she hears Patrice say "We'll give some to Mr Oakfield" this must not be obvious to the audience, who should be left in doubt Melody should not indicate to them, in any way, that she has heard these words

Page 95   While Mary-Lou's immediate subsequent actions are determined by the fact that she sees Michael take a drink from the gin bottle, this must not be obvious to the audience, who should be left with the impression that the love potion is, in fact, working Mary-Lou's observation of Michael's hurried drink should therefore be very casual

FURNITURE AND PROPERTY LIST

ACT I On stage

Bed made up with sheets, pillows, bedspread
Nightstand with bedside light
Couch
Coffee table
One or two easy chairs
Side table
Bar table
    on it bottles, including empty gin bottle, glasses, water jug,
        soft drinks, wine bottles, corkscrew
Bookcase with books, including Encyclopedias
Large iron tongs
Paintings
Bric-a-brac
Animal heads
Cow skin rug

ACT I Off stage

Tray with glasses, silverware (Melody)
Dish towel (Jarvis)
Newspaper (Patrice)
Two suitcases (Michael)
Tray with coffee pot and mugs (Melody)
Umbrella (Oakfield)
Briefcase containing papers, files (Oakfield)
Two straight chairs (Melody)
Manila envelope containing typewritten letter (Jarvis)
Thermos bottle (Jarvis)
Dish cloth (Melody)
Towels - powder room (Melody)
Towels – west wing (Melody)

Skirt, blouse, shoes (Tammy-Jo)
Carry-all (Mary-Lou)
Back Pack (Mary- Lou)
Vacuum cleaner with long cord (Melody)

ACT II   On stage
Strike coffee cups, glasses

ACT II   Off Stage
Tray with coffee cups (Jarvis)
Coffee pot (Melody)
Broom (Michael)
Meat cleaver (Melody)
Castrating shears (Melody)
Duplicate black lace teddy (Mary-Lou)
Rope (Melody)
Jumper cables (Melody)
Baseball bat (Melody)

PERSONAL
Glasses (Oakfield)
Glasses (Mary-Lou)
Purse containing pen and checkbook (Patrice)
Comb (Michael)
Two checks (Jarvis)

COSTUME PLOT

MELODY
Wrap around black skirt
White blouse
White apron
Dark hose
High-heel pumps
Black underwear and garter belt
Silk robe

JARVIS
Dark pinstripe or charcoal gray pants
White shirt with French cuffs
Dark vest and tie
Black shoes and socks

PATRICE
Two-piece suit
Blouse
High-heel shoes and hose
Raincoat
Silk pajamas
Peignoir-type robe
Slippers

MICHAEL
Raincoat
Blue blazer and gray pants
Shirt and tie
Shoes and socks
Hat
Boxer shorts

Undershirt

OAKFIELD

Business suit
Shirt and tie
Shoes and socks
Hat
Raincoat
Bathrobe
Two undershirts (one torn)
Boxer shorts with red hearts

TAMMY -JO

Checkered shirt with pockets
Blue denim skirt (long)
Cowboy boots and hat
Silver belt
Rain slicker
Skirt (knee-length)
Blouse
Shoes
Silk robe

MARY-LOU

Denim shirt
Blue jeans
Boots
Rain hat
Poncho
Bathrobe
Slippers
High-heel pumps
Black fishnet tights
Black lace teddy

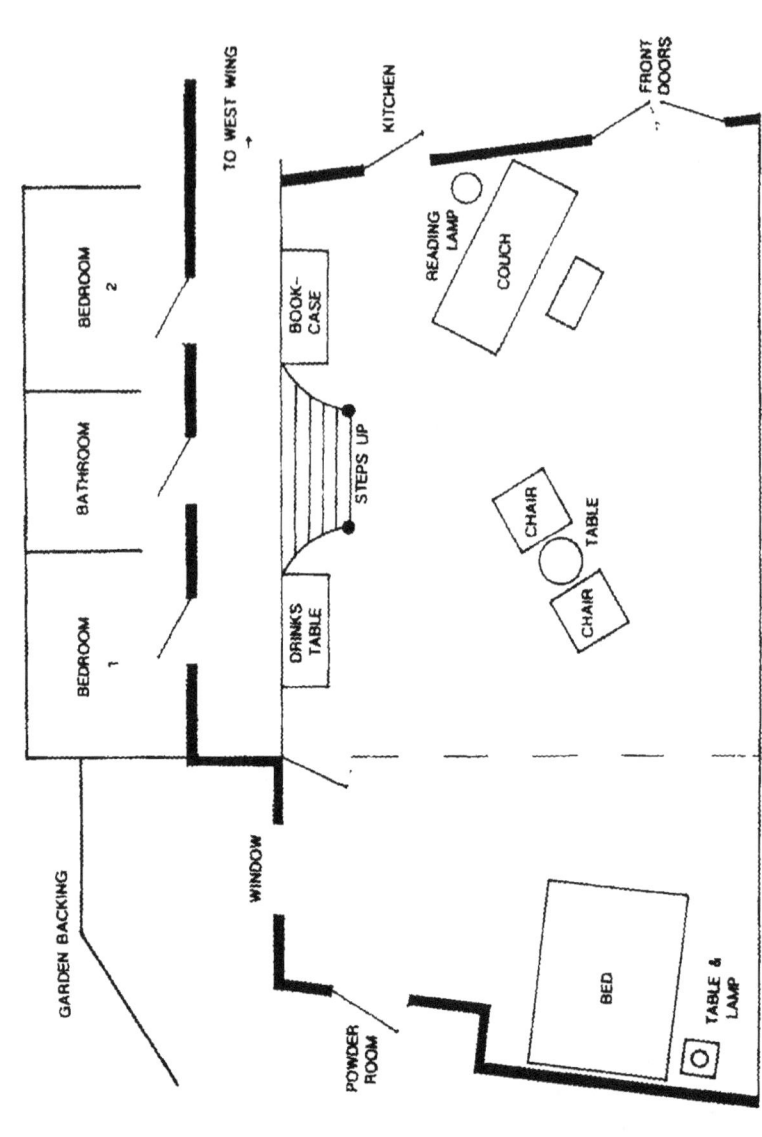

Works by
Michael Parker...

The Amorous Ambassador

Hotbed Hotel

The Lone Star Love Potion

Never Kiss a Naughty Nanny

The Sensuous Senator

There's a Burglar in My Bed

Who's in Bed with the Butler

Whose Wives Are They Anyway?

(with Susan Parker)

Sex Please We're Sixty!

Sin, Sex, and the C.I.A.

What is Susan's Secret?

Please visit our website **samuelfrench.com** for complete
descriptions and licensing information.

OTHER TITLES AVAILABLE FROM SAMUEL FRENCH

SIN, SEX & THE C.I.A.

Michael Parker and Susan Parker

Comedy / 3m, 4f

Huge oil reserves have been discovered in The Chagos Islands. O.P.E.C. is pressuring the Chagosians to join the cartel. A C.I.A. agent and an under Secretary of State, whose life appears to be run by her libido, are sent to a C.I.A. safe house in the mountains of Virginia to begin negotiations for the U.S. to place the Chagos Islands under their protection. Unfortunately, no one knows who the islands' representative really is. We are left to wonder how the C.I.A. agent ever got the job. He gets caught in all his own booby traps, he electrocutes himself, he sets fire to himself, he gets a bucket stuck on his head, and finally locks himself in his own handcuffs! Add to the inevitable chaos, a stranded televangelist, his innocent secretary (or is she?), an ex-marine caretaker, who isn't what he seems to be, and a mysterious, glamorous neighbor, and you have a complex, laugh out loud farce, that can be played on any stage.

"This play has character development, as every good play must."
"The plot has more turns than Soda Bay Road."
– *Record Bee,* Lakeport, California

"*Sin, Sex & the C.I.A.* generously incorporates every aspect of farcical comedy into its insanely funny script."
– Hemet, California

"Packed with double entendres and lot of humor"
"….comic moments and hearty laughs."
– *Sarasota Herald Tribune,* Sarasota, Florida

"Nearly every element of comic farce is present in this show – for an audience that means laughter from beginning to end!"
– Paradise Playhouse, Excelsior Springs, MO

"Laugh out loud hilarity…the laughs are relentless."
– *The Press-enterprise,* California

"Rib splittingly funny"
"A complex and hilariously funny plot"
"The Parkers are masters at this style of theatre"
– *Englewood Sun Herald,* Englewood, Florida

OTHER TITLES AVAILABLE FROM SAMUEL FRENCH

NEVER KISS A NAUGHTY NANNY

Michael Parker

Farce / 4 or 5m, 3f / Interior

Mr. Broadbent, a developer and builder, has created "THE HOUSE OF THE FUTURE". He has filled it with gadgets such as: self lighting fire places, a self cleaning bathroom, central trash disposal units, automatic closets, hidden telephones, and his masterpiece "The Personal Ion Chamber." The house, however, has remained unsold for four years, probably because, as we see in the course of the play, most of the innovations of the future fail to work properly.

He has, at last, found prospective buyers, Fred and Gladys McNicoll, and invites them to stay in the house. He is determined to offload this huge "White Elephant." He bribes two members of his staff, Casey Cody and Ben Adams, to pose as a married couple, who are renting the house. They are to extol its virtues and explain how everything works. He is pulling out all the stops. The fridge is full of expensive wine and he has hired a chef to prepare a gourmet meal. Unknown to The McNicolls', he even has his maintenance man Eddie Cott on hand to make running repairs. He thinks he has all the bases covered.

When Gladys hears Casey refer to Mr. Cott by name, the cat seems to be out of the bag, but Casey quickly recovers by saying she didn't say "Mister Cott" but "Ms. Turcotte", the children's nanny. Eddie Cott now spends the rest of the play as Nanny Turcotte. A surprise visitor, Mr. Brooks, takes an almost insane fancy to "Nanny" who now has to defend 'her' honor, as well as fix the gadgets, all of which, without exception, misbehave.

"In this play, technology that doesn't work is just plain fun. Two hours of enjoyment and laughter." – *The Seminole Beacon*, Tampa

"I was laughing so much I could barely hold the camera still." – WVTV Fox 13, Tampa - St. Petersberg

"Its many twists and turns make *Never Kiss a Naughty Nanny* a classic farce, which is sure to bring a smile." – *The Citizen*, Clearwater

SAMUELFRENCH.COM